FLETCHER

STARGAZER ALIEN MYSTERY BRIDES #2

TASHA BLACK

13TH STORY PRESS

Copyright © 2020 by 13th Story Press

All rights reserved. This book or any portion thereof may not be reproduced or used in any manner whatsoever without the express written permission of the publisher, except for the use of brief quotations in a book review.

13th Story Press

PO Box 506

Swarthmore, PA 19081

13thStoryPress@gmail.com

TASHA BLACK STARTER LIBRARY

Packed with steamy shifters, mischievous magic, billionaire superheroes, and plenty of HEAT, the Tasha Black Starter Library is the perfect way to dive into Tasha's unique brand of Romance with Bite!
Get your FREE books now at tashablack.com!

FLETCHER

1

JANA

Jana Watson was dreaming.

She knew it from the sight of the beach - the cool blue ocean and the snowy white sand, baking under a hot afternoon sun.

She had spent every summer at the same beach as a kid, until her family lost just about everything but each other in the recession.

The house at the Jersey shore was nothing special, as her mom had told her repeatedly. They'd bought it cheap, meaning to fix it up one day, but the bank took it away before they ever got the chance.

Jana didn't think about the paneled walls and the chipped Formica counters. Whenever she recalled the house "down the shore," she always remembered the creak of the porch swing, and the way the humidity made the painted floor boards cling slightly to her bare feet like kisses.

To Jana, it had been the most magical place in the world. When she made it big, she was going to buy it back, or a place just like it. Whenever things got stressful, she closed her eyes and pictured herself here.

But it never felt so real as it did right now.

The sand was hot enough to almost burn the soles of her feet, and the scent and sight of the ocean filled her with a feeling of smallness she hadn't experienced in so long.

She looked out beyond the waves at the place where the sky and sea melted into each other and shivered with delight. Jana took a step toward the water and a salty breeze whipped by, carrying her straw hat with it.

She turned to see it tumbling across the sand. And though she knew the wind and gravity alternately controlled it, it felt as if some other thing were pulling it, too. It was as if the hat were on marionette strings so that some unseen force could draw it into the tall grasses.

She chased it lazily, half-watching its progress. When it found a lively air current and sailed over her head, she spun around, back toward the beach.

The sun was sinking now, glittering on the water and setting the waves into bold relief. Its brilliance made her blink against the sight before her.

A man stood, silhouetted against the shimmering ocean.

He was holding her hat.

Jana shielded her eyes with her hand and tried got get a look at him.

The shape of him was familiar somehow. He was huge and muscular, yet his posture was not menacing.

He looked like he was waiting for her. Like he would patiently wait lifetimes…

"Fletcher?" she whispered, knowing him by his gentle presence more than his physical features. Although his sandy hair and deep blue eyes seemed like a perfect echo of their surroundings.

He moved toward her, slowly enough that she could change her mind if she wanted.

But Jana's body and soul were ready to surrender to her need for him, which felt heavy as an anchor, inexorable as the setting of the sun over the water.

"Jana," he murmured, taking her in his arms.

His chest was warm, and she could feel the flex of his muscles as his arms closed around her.

Just as she had always imagined.

She shivered with pleasure as he nuzzled her hair.

"Jana," he murmured again. "Jana."

His voice was pitching strangely higher now.

No, no, no...

"Jana."

The dream was ending. Already, she could feel her pillow wrapped in her arms instead of his strong body, the cool sheet beneath her instead of the hot sand.

"Jana, it's time to go," came Vi's impatient voice from the other side of the door.

"I'm up," Jana managed. "I'm up, just give me a minute."

"Awesome," Vi said approvingly. "You have twenty minutes."

If she had twenty minutes, Jana would have much preferred to spend it seeing where that dream was going.

But there was no point arguing with Vi. Jana's amazing roommate had made the decision to give up on her mobile pet grooming business and hang a shingle as a private detective instead. And Jana, having nothing else to do while she awaited the results of her second Broadway callback, had volunteered to be her Girl Friday.

She dragged herself out of bed and headed to her bathroom for a quick shower.

Twenty minutes later on the dot, Jana was dressed and

ready with a cup of coffee in hand, sitting at the picnic table on the shared patio behind their building.

Vi had a cup of coffee too, but she had to keep putting it down because she talked with her hands.

"It could be a very long morning," Vi was warning Jana. "We have no idea when he's going to take the tow truck out."

"Isn't that kind of the whole deal with a stakeout?" Jana asked.

"Yeah, but I wasn't sure you knew," Vi said.

"Only from the movies, but I think I'm good," Jana said. "I brought a thermos of coffee, and…" She pulled a pair of sunglasses out of her bag and slid them on. "These."

Vi burst out laughing.

"What?" Jana asked. "I just got them. You don't like them?"

"No, no, they're great," Vi said. "It's just… you're the only person I know who can put on a pair of sunglasses and look less incognito."

Well, there was nothing Jana could do about that.

"I guess it's not your fault you're gorgeous," Vi said, shaking her head. "I'm going in to grab my bag. Stay here a minute."

Jana laughed and watched her go. There was a time when that whole exchange would have given her a stomachache.

Jana was tall and curvy, even her dark eyes were larger than life. What she would have given to have her friend's less conspicuous appearance back in high school.

She had always been told she was beautiful, but a quick glance at a magazine flipped that idea on its head. Compared to those images, everything about Jana was excessive - too tall, too heavy, even too loud. Or at least that was the impression she got from them.

Ironically, it was a teenaged summer begrudgingly spent at Theatre camp because there were no spaces left at Art camp, that had given Jana the escape she needed from worrying about being herself.

At first, she had been more self-conscious than ever, standing on the stage, wishing she could disappear completely - or failing that, wishing that at least thirty percent of her could disappear.

Then Mr. Lafferty had taken notice of her. No matter what else was going on, he would call out to her, "No slouching, Jana," or "Stand tall, Jana," or, everyone's favorite, "Own it, Jana!"

And once she could stand up tall and proud on the stage while the other kids cheered her on, it was suddenly easier to picture standing up tall at home and at school. She floated through the rest of summer, loving her new lease on life.

On the last day of camp Mr. Lafferty pulled her aside.

"Jana," he said, "I'm proud of you. And I think you've got talent. You may have a future in theatre if you're willing to work hard."

"I don't know," she'd said, shrugging.

It was one thing for your school friends to tell you to own it. It was another to compete in a field full of critical strangers, where looks were everything.

"Who is the target audience in live theatre?" Mr. Lafferty had asked.

"I don't know," Jana said again, but this time with interest. She had never really thought about that. "Everyone?"

"Sure," Mr. Lafferty said. "Everyone is welcome at the theatre. But the patrons who spend the most, donate the most, and spread the word the most are women, age forty to sixty."

"Yeah?" Jana asked, wondering what he could possibly be trying to tell her.

"Women age forty to sixty don't give a damn about whether you're an emaciated waif or a curvy starlet," Mr. Lafferty said, impressing her by dropping a curse word. "They just want to see good theatre. But they have something going against them."

Yeah, women have half the world going against them, Jana thought to herself.

"Do you know what it is?" Mr. Lafferty asked.

Jana shook her head, not wanting to get drawn into an adult conversation about sexism.

"Their eyesight," he said, tapping beside his right eye with his index finger. "The world starts slowly growing dimmer and harder to see the minute you turn forty. I should know."

"Whoa," Jana said.

"Yeah," Mr. Lafferty said. "Anyway, with that crowd, your fantastic physicality and your expressive features will be like catnip. Small actors get swallowed up in a big space, but you were built for Broadway, Jana Watson."

Chills went down her spine and she grinned at him.

"Anyway, I hope you had a great summer, and don't forget," he said and paused, waiting for her to say it.

"Own it," she replied, meaning it.

"Own it, indeed," he had agreed.

The door behind her opened again, rousing Jana from her memories.

She turned to see if Vi was ready to go.

But it was Fletcher who stood in the threshold, gazing at her like she was an ice cream sandwich on a hot summer day.

Jana felt the blood rush to her cheeks. After the dream

she'd just had it was impossible to look at the handsome alien without wanting to throw herself at him.

"Good morning," Fletcher said politely.

"Good morning," she echoed.

"You are up very early," he pointed out.

He wasn't wrong. It was about five-thirty, and it felt even earlier to her.

"Vi and I are going on a stakeout," Jana told him.

"Is that like a cookout?" he asked, looking interested. "Is there steak?"

Jana suppressed a chuckle. The aliens were enormous, and they were always ready for a big meal, even a steak dinner at five-thirty in the morning.

"Not quite," Jana explained. "You know the man in town with the missing cars that we were talking about - Herman Wendall?"

"The cars that are called clunkers?" Fletcher asked.

"Yes," Jana said. "Well, we're trying to figure out who stole his old cars, and why."

"How will you do that?" Fletcher asked, sitting down across from her.

"Well, we figured it would be difficult to steal cars that aren't functional. You can't just drive them away." Jana said. "Vi did the research, and there's only one car towing company in this whole area that has a flatbed truck. So we suspect the owner may know something about the theft."

But by the time she finished explaining, she was barely registering her own words. It was just that Fletcher's eyes were so blue, and so deep. She swore she could see whole galaxies spinning in them.

The back door opened again, breaking the spell.

"Hey Fletcher," Vi said, coming out to join them. "You ready, Jana?"

"Sure," Jana said, wishing she didn't feel so regretful about leaving the big alien.

Vi's phone played an ominous piano chord.

"What is that sound?" Jana asked.

"A new auto listing," Vi said, almost dropping her phone in her eagerness to get it out of her pocket and check it out. "I set up alerts on all of the local auto-sales sites, just in case anyone tried to unload any of the cars we're looking for."

Jana was riveted. This was better than any soap opera.

"It's a match," Vi reported. "But it's almost a five-hour drive from here. It would take us all day."

"What do we do?" Jana asked.

Vi scowled.

"As much as I want to check out the tow truck driver, I think I should go check out this car. It's a more solid lead."

"I can still do the stakeout while you and Hannibal check out the car listing," Jana offered.

Vi looked torn.

"Seriously, I'll be fine," Jana said.

"I don't know this tow truck guy," Vi said. "He was very evasive when I called him. For all we know, he's got something to do with this. He could be dangerous. And besides, if you're there for hours, you really need back-up. Solo stakeouts are for advanced detectives."

"I'll go with you, Jana," Fletcher offered.

Jana's stomach did a little backflip at the thought, and she looked at Vi for her reaction.

2

FLETCHER

Fletcher watched as the two women exchanged a look.

He was not skilled in the more subtle ways of Earth yet. They might decide that he would not be a help on the stakeout. But he wasn't sure what he would do if Jana tried to go without him.

Vi had indicated this work might be dangerous, and the need to protect Jana overwhelmed him.

Jana was his mate - he knew it to his bones. But she seemed to deny their attraction, to deny his very existence at times.

It was confusing and pleasant at the same time, being near her, but unable to claim her without upsetting some unspoken rule.

The men from Aerie were attuned to unspoken rules. On Aerie, where they had existed as gaseous masses, there was very little privacy. Manners were everything when it came to keeping society together.

So although he did not understand why Jana didn't want

to talk about their connection, he respected her boundaries and did not push it.

They would join when the time was right. He was certain of it.

"You know what?" Vi said. "That's not a bad idea."

Jana smiled and looked down in a shy way that was the opposite of her usual confidence.

Fletcher wondered what it could mean. Was she ashamed to be happy to spend time with him?

"Go tell your brothers," Vi told Fletcher. "And grab anything you need for the day."

He nodded, then jogged upstairs to find Hannibal and Spenser draped over the sofa eating breakfast.

"Hello, brothers," Fletcher said.

"Hello, Fletcher," Hannibal said. "Do you want toaster waffles?"

Hannibal gestured at a plate on the coffee table. It looked like his brothers had toasted all the waffles in the box.

"I don't have time," Fletcher replied proudly. "I am going on a stakeout."

"Is that like a cookout?" Spenser asked, sitting up quickly. "Can you bring us back some steak?"

"No," Fletcher said. "That's what I thought, too. But really it's spying."

"Oh." Spenser sat back and took a bite of his waffle.

"Who are you spying on?" Hannibal asked suspiciously.

Fletcher didn't blame him. Spying was the opposite of good manners. Everyone knew that.

"A man who Vi suspects is involved in stealing those cars," Fletcher explained. "I am going with Jana, and you and Vi are going to look at another clue."

"We are?" Hannibal asked.

"And what am I doing?" Spenser asked in a grumpy way.

Fletcher's heart ached for his brother Spenser, who was having a harder time adjusting to this new world.

Spenser had not yet found a mate. And though he expressed happiness at his brothers' joy, it was clear that the big alien needed a mate of his own to ease his transition to Earth.

"Did you not promise to go to the garden store with Micah and Tony?" Hannibal asked Spenser.

"Oh, yes," Spenser remembered, looking more cheerful.

Tony had said the best hamburgers in town could be obtained at the restaurant next to the garden store. The three were planning to make a day of their excursion.

Fletcher ran to his room and grabbed his backpack. He looked around, uncertain what he was supposed to bring for a stakeout.

He decided on a warm sweater and a dictionary. Then he headed for the kitchen and grabbed a few snacks and two bottles of water and crammed those in as well.

Satisfied, he headed for the door.

"What will you and Jana be doing?" Hannibal asked.

"I think we sit in the car and watch for the man who owns the tow truck to appear," Fletcher said.

"So you will be doing almost nothing?" Hannibal asked. "For hours?"

"Uh, yes," Fletcher realized this was true.

"Are you going to talk to her?" Hannibal asked.

Spenser leaned forward again to see what Fletcher would say.

"I-I am not sure," Fletcher said. "I do not wish to frighten her. It seems that there is some barrier to our union."

"How do you know?" Hannibal asked. "Have you talked to her?"

He hadn't. But Jana was the best kind of human, the kind who wore her feelings plainly on her face, which made it easier for an alien to understand how a conversation was going.

The only times Jana made herself vague and unreadable were those moments when they were close enough to touch, when the electric attraction between them was undeniable.

It gave Fletcher the feeling that she was unready, or perhaps unwilling to be his mate.

And as much as he ached for her, it was more important to him that she feel happy. Her vibrant happiness was his favorite thing about her.

He would not be the one to rob her of any part of it.

"Go with your instinct, brother," Spenser said suddenly in his deep serious voice.

"I will," Fletcher told him gratefully, heading for the door.

"But don't wait so long that you make her think you don't want her." Hannibal cried out after him as he closed the door.

3

JANA

Jana climbed into the old ice cream truck and waited for Fletcher to join her.

"May I ask a question, Jana?" he said politely as he got in.

"Sure," she said.

He was always so straightforward. Some wild part of her brain waited for him to propose to her, or at least proposition her.

"Why are we taking the ice cream truck?" he asked.

Oh. She wasn't sure if she was disappointed or relieved.

"Vi has to drive a very long distance," Jana explained. "And this truck doesn't get good gas mileage. So she's taking my car."

Vi had fixed up the old ice cream truck to use for her mobile dog grooming business. That wasn't happening anymore, but her friend didn't really have the money to upgrade to something more economical.

"But aren't we supposed to be spying?" Fletcher asked. "This vehicle seems... conspicuous."

He wasn't wrong.

"We'll just have to park it really carefully," Jana said, hoping there was a spot big enough to hide an ice cream truck somewhere in sight of the towing lot. At least Vi had gotten around to painting over the ice cream menu on the side, so they wouldn't spend the entire time getting flagged down by a bunch of soon-to-be-disappointed kids waving change and screaming about rocket pops.

"This is a good plan, Jana," Fletcher said. "I am excited for our adventure."

He smiled at her and she instantly had butterflies in her tummy again.

She smiled back instinctively and willed herself to start the truck instead of mooning over him.

As she pulled down the alleyway and headed for the road out of town, she automatically reached for the radio.

Not knowing what Fletcher would like to listen to, she opted for the classical station on low volume. The background music might help with her nerves.

All of a sudden, she was feeling a little weird about this stakeout.

"Are you okay?" Fletcher asked, as if reading her mind.

"I don't know," she said. "I guess I'm just a little worried we'll be spotted."

"Then let's make a plan for what we'll do if that happens," Fletcher suggested sensibly.

"I guess we could say the truck broke down," Jana said slowly.

"That's a good idea," Fletcher agreed. "Now we have a plan."

She glanced over at him. He looked so content, it was almost like he was actually glowing.

It would be amazing to live such a straightforward life.

Fletcher took joy in a good meal, in helping his friends, in an afternoon in the garden.

Jana felt as if she had grown calloused from spending her whole life on Earth. She was so focused on career goals that it was hard to remember to take pleasure in the small things. It must be nice to view the world with fresh eyes.

The houses grew farther apart as they drove in companionable silence. Before long, the thin ribbon of suburb turned to farmland.

"This is near where Vi and Hannibal found the dogs," Fletcher noted.

"Yeah," Jana said. "We're going to pass the barn soon."

"Why do you think the person took those dogs?" Fletcher asked.

It was a question they all had been asking themselves.

Why would you steal someone's dogs and pay to have them trained?

"If it was only one dog, it could have been revenge," Jana mused. "Like someone was mad at another person and they took the dog but didn't want to get caught with it."

"But there were many dogs," Fletcher pointed out. "And why bother paying to train it as revenge?"

"That's the million-dollar question," Jana agreed. "It's a figure of speech," she added when she saw the confused look on his face.

He smiled in understanding.

The group of friends had been over it again and again, but they were no closer to coming up with a theory that actually made sense.

Officer West, the policewoman who met them when their landlords' dog went missing, had posed the idea that maybe the person was a big fan of the dog trainer, and had done this hoping to help him.

The trainer was Darwin Brody, a former professional football player. The theory made some loose sense, though if the person were really a fan, they surely would have wanted contact with him. There was no reason for them to remain anonymous. And the person who kidnapped the dogs had merely sent an Über driver with the dogs and an envelope of cash to Brody, asking him to train them.

So the fan theory made no sense either.

But at this point, none of their ideas really did.

Jana turned the van onto a side street and headed for the tow company.

"Okay, let's keep an eye out for a good place to set up," she told Fletcher.

Unfortunately, they seemed to be surrounded by potato fields on both sides with no place to hide.

They had nearly reached the tow company lot when Jana spotted a stand of yew trees near the roadside that might provide the cover they were hoping for.

"Here we go," she said as she pulled the truck onto the dirt road that led onto the farmland next to the trees.

"What are we doing?" Fletcher asked.

"I think we can hide between the trees," Jana said.

"Won't the owner of the farm want to know why we're here?" Fletcher asked.

"This is a fallow strawberry field," Jana said. "The owner won't even look at it again until next year. Hopefully."

Fletcher nodded.

"Okay, hold on," Jana said, hoping the ice cream truck could handle a bit of off-road action.

They bumped and banged a bit, but ended up more or less exactly behind the stand of trees. The thin branches provided modest cover, but it was still easy for them to see between the trees and branches to the towing lot across the street.

"This seems pretty good," Jana said, feeling pleased with herself. "Now we wait."

She pulled two pairs of binoculars out of her bag and handed one to Fletcher.

"What is this?" he asked, examining the binoculars.

"They're for seeing things that are far away," Jana explained. "You put them up to your eyes and then you slide the dial to help you focus on the thing you want to see."

She watched as he played with them.

He looked at things outside the car, then he tried to look at her.

"I'm ready for my close up, Mr. DeMille," she joked.

"Who is Mr. DeMille?" he asked, looking around the inside of the truck.

"Oh, it's a joke," she said. "Kind of an actor thing. Cecil DeMille was a famous director. And a close-up is when the camera shows a shot of just the actor's face."

"You are an actor," Fletcher said thoughtfully. "Or are you an actress?"

"Depends on who you ask," Jana said. "Stage performers generally prefer the term actor, even if we're female. It indicates seriousness about craft."

"Are women not serious?" Fletcher asked.

Jana's eyebrows shot up. Then she remembered how new he was to everything.

"Oh, we're dead serious," she assured him. "But there's a belief out there, and it's somewhat accurate, that most female actors are only cast in roles because of their beauty, or because the directors are attracted to them."

"Are the directors attracted to you?" Fletcher asked.

His voice was strangely rough.

"Who knows?" Jana asked. "But none of them have really hit on me yet, which makes me one of the lucky ones."

"Why would they hit you?" Fletcher sounded horrified. "Is it part of the acting?"

"Oh dear," Jana said. "To hit *on* someone means to flirt or to ask them to go on a date."

"Ah," Fletcher said, looking much relieved. "I am glad no director has hit you, or hit *on* you."

"That's one for the gratitude board," Jana agreed.

"What is the gratitude board?" Fletcher asked.

She really needed to stop mentioning things he didn't understand. It must have been a frustrating way to hold a conversation. Although to his credit, he showed no signs of impatience with her.

"A lot of people try to visualize things to make themselves feel happy or inspired by putting images on a poster board," Jana explained. "Some people make them for things they aspire to do, or for things that make them feel grateful."

"You have such a board?" Fletcher asked her.

"Not yet," she admitted. "But I always thought it sounded kind of neat. I guess I need an aspiration board to remind me to make a gratitude board."

"We will make one together," he said. "When we are finished with our stakeout."

"Oh shoot, you're right," Jana remembered. "We should totally be watching the tow lot right now."

She held up her binoculars and focused them on the lot.

The sky had taken on a pink glow, and it cast a dreamy haze over the tow lot and the big metal shop.

Jana wondered suddenly if the two missing cars could be right there in the shop.

It would be amazing if she and Fletcher somehow found the cars while Vi was away. It would be super exciting to really make something of this time while she was waiting to find out about her audition.

They watched the lot for a long time, taking turns having a coffee break.

Jana couldn't help checking her phone from time to time.

Don't think about the call-back. Don't think about the Cyndi Lauper Story, she told herself.

But it was hard not to think about what it would be like to play Cyndi at the Public.

Jana had done a handful of national tours, as well as some voiceover work and regional and off-Broadway theatre.

But this role was something completely different, something that would change her career and her life.

Sometimes she thought to herself that there were really two timelines with two Janas in them - one who got the part and started a new life in the city, and another who came close but didn't get the role.

What would it be like to go back on the road with another touring show, knowing how close she had been to breaking out in the city?

She hoped she wouldn't have to find out.

"What's that?" Fletcher asked.

She refocused her binoculars and saw movement at the gates. Sure enough, the flat bed tow truck was leaving the drive and heading out to work.

Jana scanned it, searching desperately for clues, remembering her earlier conversation with Vi.

"What will I be looking for?" Jana had asked Vi before they left.

"Clues," Vi had replied, as if it were the most obvious thing in the world.

Vi sometimes forgot that not everyone had her gift for picking up details.

"*What* clues?" Jana had asked.

"You're looking for something that doesn't belong," Vi had said. "Something unusual, something that doesn't make sense in the story of what is supposed to be happening."

Right now, all Jana saw was a flatbed tow truck.

She tried to pick out as many details as she could. The man driving it appeared to be the owner. He was wearing a flannel shirt. The truck was not clean, but not especially dirty. The bed was empty. It had a Pennsylvania license plate.

Then it was gone.

"Darn," she said to herself.

"What's wrong?" Fletcher asked.

"Nothing," she said. "And that's the trouble. Maybe Vi would have noticed something out of place, but I certainly didn't."

"It was far away and moving quickly," Fletcher said.

Vi was going to be really disappointed.

Suddenly an idea occurred to Jana.

"You know, if he's gone with the truck, he must be out to tow a car," Jana thought out loud. "Which means he won't be back for a while. Maybe we can check out the lot and the shop."

"That's a good idea," Fletcher said. "Why don't you stay here and keep a lookout and I'll go over there? You can beep the horn if he's coming back, and I'll know to hide."

"No way," Jana said. "I already can't search for clues as well as Vi, and you've got an even worse shot than I do."

He looked troubled.

"But I like your idea a lot," Jana said. "You stay here, and I'll go over there."

"Jana, this isn't a good plan," he said.

"Are you suggesting that because I'm a woman I'm incapable of doing something risky?" she asked lightly.

His face went blank.

"I'm sorry, Jana, if this is what you wish, I will help you."

She felt a pang of guilt.

But there was no time to waste explaining herself.

"Perfect," she said. "Keep a sharp eye out. I'll be right back."

4
JANA

Jana slipped out of the truck, trying not to think about hurting Fletcher's feelings. Just because his body made him look like a man, and wow did it ever, didn't mean he knew the ins and outs of sexism on Earth.

She would be done and back before he had a chance to lick his wounds, she decided. They could talk more about it then.

She carefully looked both ways before crossing the road, though she would have been able to see a car in either direction for at least a mile.

When she reached the gravel drive to the towing lot, she saw a huge metal mailbox with a lock on it - probably the lockbox for mail and keys when customers dropped off after hours.

She jogged past it and headed for the lot.

It had looked mostly empty from the road and indeed there were only few cars in the dirt parking area. None of them matched what she was looking for.

She took a deep breath and headed for the shop.

It was as big as an airplane hangar, its metal walls painted light blue with the towing company's logo of a tow truck with a smiling front bumper and eyes with stars in them on its windshield. *Stargazer Bill's Towing* was emblazoned above the image in a half-circle.

She tried the front door and was unsurprised to find it locked.

She checked her phone. It had been just over five minutes since they'd seen the man drive away. She headed into the tall weeds next to the shop to see if there was a side door.

The grass tickled her shins, and the sun was bright overhead, glaring on the dusty shop windows. She tried peering in but it was too dark inside and too bright outside for her to see much.

When she had almost reached the rear of the building, she heard a tinkling, jaunty music playing in the distance. It was so out of place that it took her a few seconds to realize what it was.

The ice cream truck song.

Fletcher must have pressed the song button instead of the horn. The owner must have returned earlier than they thought he would.

Her heart dropped to her stomach and she darted behind the shop to try and figure out what to do.

She had thought before that it would be easy to hide, but the shop and the grass were the only things out here, besides the driver's little house which was a good distance behind the lot.

On instinct, she tried the back door of the shop.
Locked.

She peered around the building and saw the flatbed truck was stopped at the lockbox by the driveway entry. The owner must be checking his mail.

Which meant she had maybe a minute before he headed back into the lot.

There was a late model sedan on the flat bed. It must have come from somewhere pretty close by. But it was work, which meant he would head to the lot or the shop.

That left Jana with only one choice. She had to hide behind the house and hope for the best.

She looked out past the shop, across the huge lot and all the way over at the house.

Glad I have long legs...

She took off like a bullet, not looking to see if she had been spotted, and pumped her legs as fast as she could.

It took at least thirty adrenaline-fueled seconds to reach the backyard of the little brick house, but it felt like forever out in the open.

She leaned against the wall, panting.

Now what?

She could hear the truck easing its way up the drive now. He hadn't shouted or honked at her, so hopefully he hadn't seen her.

But how was she supposed to get back across the street and over to the ice cream truck with him directly between her and her destination?

She certainly couldn't hide out behind the man's house all day. And she couldn't even really peek out to plot a route without exposing herself.

Just as she began to feel she was really in too deep, she spotted movement on the road in the opposite direction of the shop.

The ice cream truck.

Holy crap.

She was pretty sure Fletcher had never driven an Earth vehicle before.

But he had managed to pull that ungainly ice cream truck back onto the road to save her.

She took off to meet him, running as fast as her legs would carry her. She was going to be sore tonight.

But something about running toward Fletcher made her feel like she could keep up the pace as long as she needed to.

5

FLETCHER

Fletcher managed to pull the truck to the side of the road.

The going was very bumpy along the dirt shoulder, but the vehicle had predictably straightforward controls.

"Fletcher," Jana cried as she wrenched open the door and stumbled into the van.

He pulled back onto the road as she yanked the door shut behind her.

The next thing he knew, she was wrapping her arms around his neck and pressing her lips to his jaw.

His body was shot through with a wave of need for his mate, amping up his senses. He was drunk on the scent of her shampoo. He could see colors outside the spectrum of the rainbow.

Jana gasped and let go of him quickly, then buckled into her seatbelt, leaving him reeling.

"I can't believe you're driving this thing," she laughed awkwardly.

He willed his body to cool and calm. If he was overwhelmed at her touch, he could only imagine how she was feeling. She could not have expected the shock of desire the mate bond would bring.

"Everyone in this van who has mastered intergalactic space travel, raise your hand," Fletcher said, winking at her and hoping to make her feel more at home.

"Are you... quoting *The Simpsons*?" she asked.

"Dr. Bhimani showed us clips from many television shows and movies that depict aliens," he explained. "She wanted us to be prepared for the preconceived notions we might experience in the world."

"Well, touché, that was a great quote," Jana said. "And I'm going to go out on a limb and say I'm impressed with your driving anyway, because I'll bet your intergalactic vehicles are more responsive than this beast."

"Just a little," he said with a smile.

It wouldn't be polite to tell her that not only were the ships from Aerie worlds more responsive than this simple contraption, but they had a biological component that bonded with their pilots allowing them to heal themselves and even to learn.

"You were very brave," he told her instead. "I have never felt such fear as when the man's truck returned. Please do not make me abandon you in a time of crisis again."

"You didn't abandon me, you rescued me," she retorted.

"Next time, I will be beside you," he assured her.

He glanced over at her and their eyes locked for a moment.

She shook her head as if to clear it. "There won't be a next time. Even up close I couldn't find any clues. The shop was locked, and he got home before I could check on the house."

That was too bad. Fletcher knew Jana had been hoping to report back to her friend with some progress.

"I'm sorry," he told her. "I will help you brainstorm ways to help Vi."

"Thanks, Fletcher," she said. "I'm sure Vi will figure everything out when she and Hannibal get back. I just thought it would be cool if I could surprise her for once."

He shrugged and kept his eyes on the road, giving her time to elaborate, or change the subject.

All he could think of was the way his cheek burned from her kiss and the need to tell her, to claim her...

"What are you thinking about?" she asked suddenly.

"I will tell you when we get home," he told her.

He had never called the apartment home before. Until now, the rough crags of Aerie were the place he thought of as his home.

But now that he and his mate both dwelled in the brick building in the village he felt the concept of home more acutely than he had ever understood it before, and he began to realize it was about much more than a physical location.

They pulled into the alleyway, where he carefully parked the truck and leapt out so that he could open Jana's door for her, just like he'd seen in the movies.

"Thank you," she said.

He stepped back slightly, anticipating the warmth he would feel when she stepped down and was close to him for a sweet moment.

But instead, she practically flung herself out of the truck and made a dash for the garden.

He followed her slowly, giving her time. If she chose to go upstairs instead of talking with him, he would allow it without complaint.

She was his mate. She could have as much time as she needed.

But when he followed her through the gate, he found her sitting on a stone bench under a small weeping cherry tree in the corner of the garden that was furthest from the house.

He was cheered inwardly. Whether she'd meant to or not, she had chosen a private spot, a romantic one, too.

"So what were you thinking about in the car?" she asked.

He took a deep breath and then knelt before her.

She blinked at him, her lips parted slightly.

Focus, Fletcher, he told himself. *Don't get distracted by her beauty and mess this up.*

It should not be possible to mess things up with a true mate. The mate bond was too strong for that.

But in this moment, to Fletcher, it seemed that there were a million ways for him to get this wrong, and only one in which she would flow into his arms and make him the happiest man on Earth.

"Jana, how much do you know about my kind?" he asked carefully.

"I know you are from Aerie," she said. "I know your gaseous form was placed in this lab-grown human body, and that you are here to know our people better."

"Yes," he agreed. "All of this is true. Do you know about our mate bonds?"

She looked down at her hands in her lap in an uncharacteristically shy manner.

"I will tell you," he said, wanting to spare her the embarrassment, though he could tell by her demeanor that she already knew. "Though my form was designed to stoke female desire, I will know only one woman in that way - my bonded mate. If my bonded mate accepts me as her own, I will give her pleasure, protection and love for the rest of our lives."

Jana was still studying her own hands, but he could feel through the tenuous bond he already shared with her that she was listening for all she was worth.

"And my mate will give me true humanity," he went on. "When we make love, I will *click* into this human body permanently, instead of merely inhabiting it temporarily. And I will be able to enjoy a full life here on Earth."

He reached out and gently placed one hand on hers.

She looked up at him, and he was grateful that he could gaze into her eyes as he said this next, most important part.

"Jana Watson," he said. "You are my true mate. You are the one who makes my soul sing. I have felt the tug of your bond on my heart since the day we met. I will not rush you to make a decision, but if you will accept me, I will make it my life's mission to bring you peace and happiness."

She looked down at their hands together on her lap.

For a moment he felt a great hope soar in his heart.

Then she looked up at him again with tears in her eyes.

"Oh Fletcher," she said sadly.

His chest seemed to cave in on itself.

"I did not mean to frighten you," he murmured.

"I'm not frightened," she said. "I'm moved. But I can't be your mate."

"Are you promised to another?" he asked.

"No," she said. "But I made a promise to myself. I promised that I would never let go of my dreams. And right now my dreams are so close I can touch them."

"Your audition?" he asked.

She nodded.

He knew that she was an actor, and that the part she wanted to play was an important one.

He had not realized that accepting it would preclude her from having a mate. Perhaps this kind of work required a vow of chastity, as some of the spiritual paths he had learned about. The arts were important on this planet, but he had not realized how important.

Whatever the reason, he would not interfere with her wishes, even though the pain he already felt was almost unbearable.

"I understand, Jana Watson," he said carefully. "I will not stand in the way of your dreams."

He got up slowly and headed back into the house, determined to hold himself together until he was out of her sight.

6

JANA

Jana spent the rest of the day in a haze.

She did all her laundry, then she washed every dish in the sink and some of the ones in the cupboard to be sure. She vacuumed and dusted and even washed the insides of all the windows.

Then she put a whole chicken in the oven with potatoes and onions and carrots.

While it baked, she showered and dressed carefully.

When she emerged from the steamy bathroom, to her sparkling apartment and the savory scent of her dinner, she knew there was nothing left to do but face her feelings.

She sat down at the kitchen table and steepled her fingers together to give herself a stern talking-to.

"Jana Watson, you made yourself a promise years ago," she told herself firmly. "You said you would never put a man in front of your career."

But he's not actually a man, a little voice inside her pointed out.

"No time for technicalities. He may not be a man yet, but he's trying to be one, and more to the point, he's at your doorstep in the wake of the biggest break of your career," she told herself. "This is exactly what you planned for. You said you wouldn't be one of the actors who quits at age thirty to have babies. You said you were in this for the long haul."

He didn't ask for babies...

"It's part of the deal," she said. "You read the articles. You know they were told to have families and settle in."

What about that movie star who met an alien at Comic Con? He travels with her.

"She's a movie star, she can afford to support an entourage," Jana told herself. "Broadway minimum won't even be enough for your own studio apartment."

But he loves me...

She stood, unable to argue with herself anymore.

What could she possibly say to that?

There would always be a little voice telling her it was okay to eat another brownie, to stay up a little later, to rehearse a little less, and now it was telling her to bond herself to an alien.

But Jana knew better.

Surrendering to your urges was unacceptable when you had a dream to focus on. That was how all the other women in acting school had fallen out of the business. It happened pleasantly - because of a boy or a cushy day job or a car payment on the pretty little coupe you just had to have.

She was too close to let it go now.

Fletcher was just going to have to find another woman.

Her heart ached, but there was relief in having decided.

She grabbed oven mitts and pulled the chicken from the oven.

It was utter perfection, gleaming with juices. The veggies were soaked in the run-off, and though she couldn't see it, she knew the stuffing hidden inside would be the best part of all.

She froze in place without closing the oven.

Hidden inside...

She might not have fully solved her heartache problem, but Jana thought she just might have solved her tow truck investigation dilemma.

7

FLETCHER

Fletcher was alternately reading a copy of *The Complete Works of William Shakespeare* and staring out the window at the birds making a nest in the gutter of the house across the street.

He had hoped that by reading the immortal words of one of Earth's greatest playwrights, he might better understand the needs of his mate.

The words in the book were beautiful, but they seemed alternately shortened and lengthened from the words Fletcher had learned. And they were strung together in a strange rhythm that made him half-hypnotized and sleepy.

The birds in the gutter, on the other hand, were extremely industrious. They busied themselves preparing their nest with a heady zeal.

Fletcher envied them. Birds were also pair-bonded, which made him feel a kinship with them.

These two had their whole lives to look forward to: hunting for bugs, flying under the bright sun, and raising the tiny hatchlings who would occupy their nest.

Fletcher had no idea how he would spend the rest of his life.

He was bonded to Jana whether she would allow herself to accept him or not. There would be no other mate.

A loud knock at the door roused him from his reverie.

Spenser, who had been sitting on the loveseat, scowling at a crossword puzzle, lurched out of his seat to answer it.

Jana stood in the doorway, looking excited.

"I need your help, guys," she said. "I have an idea. Also I cooked a chicken."

"A chicken?" Spenser said with interest.

"Yes, yes, come on," she told him.

Fletcher got up right away. He and his brother trailed up the stairs after her.

The scent of delicious food greeted them before they even reached the landing.

Spenser turned back and gave Fletcher a look, as if to say that he could not believe how good it smelled. It was hard to disagree.

Jana opened the door and they followed her inside.

Where the aliens' apartment was lightly furnished and spare, Vi and Jana's place was made cozy by extraneous items.

All the shelves were filled to overflowing with books. The tables were laden with coasters and napkins and magazines. Framed posters and paintings adorned nearly every wall.

But the place was still very tidy, somehow, in spite of its rich population of items.

Fletcher felt at home right away.

"Come on," Jana said, gesturing for them to follow her into the kitchen. "We can talk while we eat."

The table was set for three, as if she had known they would decide to join her. Fletcher smiled at the thought.

They all sat, and Jana served out generous portions of the meal.

Fletcher waited for her to sit before he began but Spenser dug right in.

"My God, woman, this is delicious," Spenser declared.

"Well, don't get any big ideas about my skills in the kitchen," Jana said dismissively. "This is one of like three things I know how to cook."

"This is enough," Spenser said, tucking in again.

Jana smiled at Fletcher and he smiled back helplessly.

"Please, eat," she said. "I'll tell you my plan when we're done."

The food was so good that it seemed to practically melt in his mouth. Too soon, his plate was empty and his belly was full.

"That was amazing," he told Jana simply. "Thank you very much."

"My pleasure," she said lightly.

"What do you need our help with?" Fletcher asked.

"Okay, so I had this crazy thought while I was cooking," Jana said, sitting back in her seat. "What if we called the tow company and got them to tow the ice cream truck into the shop?"

"How would that get us clues?" Fletcher asked.

"What if we were hiding in it?" Jana asked, her eyes sparkling.

"Oh, that sounds clever," Spenser said, his eyebrows slightly raised.

"It sounds dangerous," Fletcher said reflexively.

"I'm not offering to do it alone," Jana said.

He eyed her, hating himself for wondering if this meant she was honoring his need to protect her.

She doesn't want you. Let her be.

And he would. But it was impossible to keep his thoughts calm when she was looking at him with her eyes dancing like that.

"That's true," he allowed. "We could go together."

"Why would that towing company take the truck?" Spenser asked sensibly.

"Cars often get towed when they're parked illegally, like in a hospital zone," Jana said. "And it's such a monstrosity that it would definitely take a flatbed truck to move it. And we know Stargazer Bill's is only shop for miles that has one of those."

"So you will park the truck in a hospital zone, and I will call the police to report it," Spenser offered quickly. "Perhaps Officer West will answer."

"Maybe," Jana agreed, giving him a funny look.

Maybe Jana had not noticed the way Spenser regarded the stern officer of the Stargazer police force, but Fletcher had.

"What is a hospital zone?" Fletcher asked.

"It's the area near a hospital, so parking there could prevent someone very sick from being seen by a doctor as quickly as possible," Jana said. "Which is why I think we'd better not do it. Not to mention that if we're breaking the law, the truck would be towed to an impound lot, not to Stargazer Bill's. And the whole point is for us to be sure we get into that shop."

"So we should smash the truck?" Fletcher asked. "Then he would bring it in to be repaired?"

"That would work," Jana nodded. "But it's too extreme.

It's not even my truck. Vi would be pretty upset if we made her insurance costs go up."

"Insurance costs?" Spenser asked.

"Too complicated, I'll explain it later," Jana said. "Long and short of it is, we can't crash the car. I guess we just need something to go wrong with it mechanically, so that it needs to go into the shop."

Fletcher had a sudden revelation. Maybe he could help after all.

"What if the steering wheel disappeared?" he asked.

"What?" Jana asked.

"It would reappear again before Vi returned," Fletcher explained. "But would it work?"

"Well, uh yeah, but how do we get the steering wheel out?" Jana asked. "I wouldn't even know where to begin."

Fletcher hesitated.

Dr. Bhimani had told the men not to reveal their gifts to humans, except for their mates.

Jana was surely his mate, but she did not intend to accept him. He was sure he was not supposed to show her what he could do with his talents.

"Don't worry," he told her instead. "Just leave it to me."

She studied his face for a moment, and must have liked what she saw in his eyes.

"Okay," she said, nodding. "Let's do it."

8

JANA

An hour later, the plan was underway.

Jana drove through the village and into the farmland again, heading for the country road near the towing company. Fletcher kept watch from the passenger seat.

Spenser had stayed at home, with his eye on the clock. When twenty minutes had passed, he would call the Stargazer Police Department. Jana had offered to just do it from her mobile phone, but he had been very insistent.

"This looks perfect," Jana said, pulling over onto the shoulder in a place wide enough that the flatbed could safely tow them away.

"Are you sure you want to do this?" Fletcher asked.

"Very sure," Jana said. "I think we might be able to get real information this way."

Fletcher nodded, though he looked concerned.

"So, what are you going to do to the steering wheel?" Jana asked, hoping he wasn't going to wrench it off the dash. He looked like he might actually be strong enough to do that.

"I promise this will not ruin the truck," Fletcher told her.

She nodded.

Fletcher touched the steering wheel and before Jana's eyes it seemed to disappear.

"H-how did you do that?" she asked.

"It is my gift," he said simply.

"What do you mean? Where did it go?" she asked.

"It went... somewhere else," he said. "A place I can retrieve it from later."

"Where?" she asked.

"It may be hard to believe," he said. "But it is on Aerie, a tiny spot on Aerie, where I can place something if I need to."

"Can everyone from Aerie do that?" she asked.

"No," he replied. "Just me, as far I know. Each of us is blessed with a unique gift. This is mine."

"Is it very difficult to do?" she asked, still amazed by what she had just witnessed.

"No," he told her, shaking his head. "It is very easy and practical. Like putting something in your pocket and taking it out again."

He made a movement as if he were grabbing something out of the air and the steering wheel reappeared. Then he vanished it once more.

She opened her mouth and closed it again. She wasn't sure why anything about this man should surprise her.

"That's amazing," she said at last. "And it's especially perfect for this situation."

His worried expression melted into a sunny smile. "I am glad you are pleased, Jana Watson."

"And if this doesn't work out," she joked, "you have a fabulous career ahead of you as a stage magician."

They shared a laugh, but it was cut short when Jana remembered their mission.

"Shoot, we should get hidden," she told him. "Spenser will have already called it in at this point."

They climbed into the back area of the truck.

Jana had built them a sort of fort out of empty boxes to make it easy for them to hide. She doubted that Bill would check out the cargo area, but it was better to be safe than sorry.

She curled up in the corner of the construction, and Fletcher joined her.

"It won't be long now," she told him, glancing at the time on her phone.

They sat in silence for a few minutes.

Jana was hyper aware of Fletcher's big body beside her, and she wondered if he felt the same shimmering waves of attraction in the air between them.

Focus, Jana, she scolded herself.

But it was very hard to focus.

The sound of an approaching engine mercifully distracted her from her thoughts exploring his big body the way her hands yearned to do.

"Is that Stargazer Bill?" Fletcher whispered.

"Probably," Jana whispered back.

There were crunching footsteps in the gravel leading up to the truck.

Jana had just enough time to realize all the holes in her plan, primarily that they had left the truck unlocked on the side of the road and anyone could have come upon it.

The driver's side door opened with a bang.

Jana jumped slightly and Fletcher grabbed her hand and gave it a gentle squeeze.

Instantly she felt a wave of endorphins rush through her.

"Damn," a masculine voice muttered. "How'd he even do that?"

Jana breathed a sigh of relief. It was obviously Bill.

They listened as the man went through the process of getting the truck prepared to go on the flatbed.

When the bumps and screeches of the truck's ascent began, Jana closed her eyes and clung harder to Fletcher's hand.

At last they were moving again.

Though she knew they were only a few minutes away from the shop, the drive seemed to take forever.

Fletcher, seeming to divine her nervousness, let go of her hand and put his arm around her.

She leaned into him, imbibing his masculine scent, feeling more at peace in spite of herself.

At last they stopped.

There was movement outside, and the sound of something opening, hopefully the door to the shop.

Then they were moving again, but very slowly.

When they came to a stop, there was the sound of a vehicle door closing.

Then there was the louder echo of a larger door closing.

In the darkness Jana, couldn't see Fletcher, but she felt him waiting in anticipation, just as she was. She didn't dare use the flashlight on her phone for fear that it would give them away if Bill was still inside the shop with them.

"Five minutes," she whispered in his ear.

She slid her phone out and even just the light from the screen was almost blinding in the total darkness. She set a timer to go off on vibrate and then put it back in her pocket.

Fletcher pulled her in close again and she allowed herself to relax against his big chest.

If they waited like this for five minutes and didn't hear

another sound, they could be fairly certain that Bill had gone back to his house for the night.

Then they could look for clues.

Assuming that Jana could restrain her desire to kiss the big alien.

He was so huge and so warm, his muscles firm against her.

She felt as if her own heartbeat had assimilated to the rhythm of his.

He let out a long, slow breath, as if he was also having a hard time staying in control.

After what felt like an eternity, the phone buzzed in her pocket.

"Okay," she whispered, turning it off.

Fletcher got up first and moved the boxes away, placing them carefully so that they could hide again in a hurry if they needed to.

Then he offered her a hand so she could scramble over them.

She headed for the front of the truck, where she rolled down the old, manually cranked window, then climbed onto the seat and lowered herself out the window, completely forgetting that the truck was still on the flatbed.

She hung in the air for a moment, legs dangling a few feet off the concrete floor of the shop. There was really nowhere else to go, so she released her grip and braced herself for the impact. Somehow, she landed on the hard surface without making too much noise, and without hurting herself.

She breathed a sigh of relief, hoping she hadn't used up all her luck for the night.

"You're up pretty high," she whispered to Fletcher.

He hopped out gracefully behind her, landing in a crouch like a cat or a superhero.

"Nice," she whispered to him.

She pulled out her phone and turned on the flashlight mode.

"Keep it low," Fletcher whispered. "So the light isn't noticeable from outside."

"Good thinking," she whispered back.

"What are we looking for?" he asked.

"Something out of place," she said, turning back to the flat bed.

Straps held the ice cream truck's wheels in place, and they rubbed the body of the truck in one spot.

She lifted the flashlight to get a better look at the straps.

They appeared to be pretty scuffed up and soiled. It made sense, it wasn't like you washed your car in preparation for a tow truck to pick it up.

She walked around the whole truck and on the last strap she saw something out of place.

"Wow," she murmured.

"What is it?" Fletcher asked.

"Look," she said. "Purple paint. The old Corvette that was stolen was purple."

"Are a lot of cars purple?" Fletcher asked.

"No," Jana said. "And this must have been from a recent tow or it would be covered over in dirt. This is the truck that moved that car."

She snapped a picture with her phone, then a longer shot that showed the whole truck, including the logo on the door.

"Now what?" Fletcher asked.

"We still don't know if he stole the cars himself, or if someone hired him," Jana pointed out.

"Like the dognapper and the trainer," Fletcher said.

"Exactly," Jana agreed. "We need to find out whether someone hired him the night the cars disappeared. He must keep some records around here somewhere."

They scanned the shop.

In one corner there was a desk covered in papers and folders as well as a small lamp.

Jana strode over with Fletcher by her side.

A light blue canvas bound book with the word *Schedule* embossed on the cover sat on the top of the desk.

Jana stared at it in amazement, unable to believe her luck.

Could it really be that easy?

She reached for it, but before she had a chance to pick it up, the door to the shop opened with a bang and she was blinded by the incoming beam of a powerful flashlight.

9

FLETCHER

Fletcher moved swiftly toward the desk, and then put his big body between Jana and the light coming from the doorway.

"Stop right there," a commanding female voice shouted. "Hands where I can see them."

He lifted his hands instinctively.

Suddenly, the overhead lights came on and the whole shop was illuminated.

He spotted Officer West, her dark eyes glaring at him suspiciously.

She lowered her flashlight and strode over, shaking her head.

"Why did I know exactly who I was going to find in here?" she asked. "It's bad enough you can't keep yourselves out of police business. Now you're breaking and entering?"

Stargazer Bill stood behind her, a furious expression on his face.

"I left something in the van," Jana blurted. "I had to come back and get it."

"Why didn't you just call me, lady?" Bill demanded.

"It was so late at night," Jana said. "I felt terrible about bothering you in the first place about the breakdown. I thought I could just slip in and grab my wallet and go."

"I just parked this thing five minutes ago," Bill said. "Then two seconds later you tripped my silent alarm."

"I didn't know that," she replied. "A friend called the breakdown in for me. He must not have called you right away."

Bill just grumbled in response.

"Come on," Officer West said. "You can explain it down at the station."

Fletcher allowed her to cuff his wrists.

It was harder to watch her cuff Jana's.

Officer West led them out to her police car. The lights were flashing red, white, and blue.

"Get in," she said.

Fletcher got in first and then Jana followed. It was more difficult to get into a car without his hands than he expected.

The officer closed and locked the door, then headed back to the doorway of the shop to talk with Bill.

"I'm so sorry, Jana," Fletcher told her. "I will not allow them to imprison you. I will find a way to get you out."

"I don't think we're going to prison for this," Jana said uncertainly. "But whatever happens, just stay calm and be polite. Don't worry about me, and please don't try to break us out. That kind of thing is just for the movies."

"Very well," Fletcher agreed, hoping she was right.

Officer West reappeared and opened the door.

"Get out," she said.

Jana slipped out and Fletcher followed her.

"You're very lucky the owner decided not to press

charges," Officer West said, unlocking Jana's handcuffs. "But the two of you need to stay out of trouble from here on in."

"Yes, ma'am," Jana said.

Officer West glared at her and then turned to Fletcher to remove his cuffs.

"Thank you," he said politely.

"You're welcome," she said. "Now get out of here before Bill changes his mind."

"Um, quick question," Jana said. "Any way you can give us a ride home? We're not too far from the station."

Officer West looked back and forth between them.

"How did you *get* here?" she asked.

"We took the bus," Jana said.

"We walked," Fletcher said at the same time.

Officer's West's eyes widened.

"We walked to the bus stop," Jana clarified. "Then we took the bus and walked here from the nearest stop. But the bus isn't running anymore."

"Just get back in," Officer West said, rolling her eyes.

The ride home seemed to go on forever. Fletcher watched the scenery pass by outside the window, eager to get home and show Jana his surprise.

At last they pulled up out front of 221B.

Spenser stood on the sidewalk, looking serious as ever as the police car pulled up.

His face brightened, however, when Officer West hopped out.

Fletcher and Jana slunk quietly out of the car.

"Hello," Spenser said a little too loudly.

"Are you," Officer West glanced at her notepad, "Spenser?"

"I am," he said.

"You called the towing company about the ice cream truck?" she asked.

"Yes," he said.

"Next time, just call again if something gets left in the truck," Officer West scolded him. "Don't let your friend do something stupid, like break into private property."

"I will, and I will not," he said politely.

She opened her mouth as if to yell at him some more and then she closed it again.

In the circle of light from the streetlamp, Fletcher could see the exact moment her features softened while gazing up at his brother's face. He'd thought Spenser's interest in the officer had been misplaced, but now he wasn't so sure.

"Come on," he whispered to Jana, taking her hand.

They slipped inside and headed up the stairs.

"What was that about?" Jana whispered.

"I think Spenser may have met his mate," Fletcher said happily.

"If that's the case, I feel sorry for him," Jana said. "I'm pretty sure she hates all of us."

"Not for long," Fletcher predicted.

"That's a nice thought," Jana said. "You want to come up and have a snack? I'm famished after all that excitement."

"Yes, please," Fletcher replied. "And I have a surprise for you."

"When could you possibly have had time to do anything to surprise me?" Jana asked. "We've been together all night."

"Just wait and see," Fletcher said.

They passed the landing for the second floor and continued up to Jana and Vi's apartment.

Jana opened the door and once again, Fletcher was transported by the good smells and interesting possessions.

"What's the surprise?" Jana asked, sitting on the sofa. "I

need some cheering up. I can't believe that whole thing was a bust."

He sat down beside her. "You know how I can place an item in another dimension?" he asked.

"Yes, your inter-dimensional pocket," Jana said.

He reached inside and grabbed hold of the item he had hidden earlier.

Jana's eyes sparkled as she watched, so he pulled it out with a little flourish.

"The schedule book," Jana breathed, accepting it from him and gazing down at it as if she couldn't' believe it was real. "How did you do it?"

"I was behind you when Officer West opened the door," he said. "I put it in my... pocket as I moved to protect you."

"I noticed that you moved in front of me," Jana said. "You risked your life to do that. Is that part of the whole mate thing?"

She sounded almost hopeful, but that didn't make sense.

"It is," he explained. "But I would have done it anyway. I care about you, Jana, beyond the mating bond. You are my friend."

Jana put the book on the coffee table and leaned forward.

Then everything seemed to move in slow motion.

He noticed the way her hair skimmed her shoulder as she moved, the slow close of her eyes, lashes kissing her cheeks just before she pressed her mouth to his.

Sensations of pain and ecstasy threatened to split him in half.

She wanted him, but she didn't want him. Her touch awoke emotions in him that he hadn't known existed.

He kissed her back, loving the taste of her lips, the scent

of her hair. He cupped her cheek in his hand and deepened the kiss instinctively.

Jana pulled back, panting slightly.

"I am sorry," he said, not remembering why he should be sorry, but knowing that something was amiss.

"Don't be," she said and kissed him again.

This time he knew what was coming and braced himself against the onslaught of sensation.

He was able to notice the sweet taste of her tongue, the tickle of her hair against his cheek, the warmth of her arms encircling his neck.

She seemed to melt into him, the softness of her small body becoming one with his larger one.

Desire licked at him like flames.

He knew he should pull back, slow down.

But the way she moved against him told him what she needed.

She was his mate, even if he could not claim her, he would not leave her wanting.

He wrapped his arms around her and carried her through the dining room and kitchen, back to the bedroom above his own.

Jana clung to him, pressing her lips to the place where his neck met his shoulder, sending shivers of need through him.

At last he reached her bed and placed her down gently and crawled in beside her.

"Fletcher," she murmured, reaching for him.

"Jana Watson, I adore you," he told her. "But I will not claim you if you do not crave our bond."

"I-I don't know what I want," she murmured, unable to meet his eyes for a moment.

It nearly broke him to see his mate, usually so definite and impassioned, looking so confused.

"The strength of the bond makes it too difficult to resist our attraction," he told her tenderly. "I will satisfy your need, but I will not claim you."

He bent to press his lips to hers and all her uncertainty melted into passion.

She kissed him back like her life depended on it.

Waves of lust shook him to his core and he clung to her, begging a higher power for the strength to give her what she craved without breaking his resolve.

He fed on her lips for a long time, stroking her hair, her arm, her belly.

When she moaned and wiggled under his hand, he kissed his way down her throat and nuzzled her collarbone as he fought with the buttons on her shirt.

She slid her hands between them, unbuttoning her shirt easily, then unclasping her undergarment and exposing her breasts for him.

He pulled back slightly to take in the sight of her.

Jana gazed up at him, her eyes hazy with lust. Her breasts were exquisite, brown-tipped nipples pebbled as if pleading for his kisses.

He lowered his face and flicked one with his tongue.

Jana whimpered and arched her back slightly.

Fletcher felt his own body respond, a demand so fierce it nearly overwhelmed him.

He clasped one of her breasts gently in his hand as he lapped and suckled at the other, drowning out the scream of his own need by stoking hers.

10

JANA

Jana let her head fall back against the pillow.

Fletcher was setting her on fire with need.

The past and the future were gone, and she couldn't remember a moment when her whole body wasn't pulled toward him like a magnet, pulsing with need.

He ravished her breasts with abandon, seeming to understand instinctively the perfect pressure and suction that made her wild.

At last, he nuzzled her belly and unclasped her jeans.

She lifted her hips, helping him ease her jeans and panties down and off.

Jana was not a small woman, allowing someone to see her naked wasn't always easy.

But Fletcher's hungry gaze told her all she needed to know about how she looked to him. It was almost like she could feel his admiration and desire through the bond he had described.

My mate...

But he crawled lower, nudging her thighs apart before

she could finish the thought. And then his mouth was on her, teasing and lavishing her, sending her halfway into madness.

"Please," she whimpered, clutching the sheets.

He responded with a storm of feverish flicks and strokes of his tongue.

Suddenly she was flying, up, up out of her body and then crashing down in endless waves of ecstasy.

When at last it was over, he crawled up beside her and pulled her into his strong arms.

She stroked his chest, and felt him respond with a restrained shudder.

He took her hand and kissed the palm. "Go to sleep, my love," he whispered.

"But..."

"I will not claim you until it is what you choose," he told her. "But I will hold and protect you."

She wanted to protest, to insist on giving him some taste of the pleasure he had sated her with.

But he held her close and stroked her back so gently that she felt sleep stealing her away in spite of herself.

11

FLETCHER

Fletcher awoke to the sound of Jana singing in the shower.

He closed his eyes again and summoned up a memory of last night.

It was hard to believe that he had been permitted to touch her, to give her such pleasure, to sleep with her wrapped in his arms.

Jana's lovely voice echoed on the tiles of the bathroom. She was happy too, he could tell by the sound. Though singing in the shower was a common human occurrence, according to the movies, Jana was skilled at singing and the beauty of her voice combined with the joy of her expression brought tears to Fletcher's eyes.

He had known of "happy crying," but never experienced it before.

Suddenly, she was emerging from the bathroom.

He noticed sadly that she was dressed. But she was smiling at him, which was a consolation.

"Hey, I'm glad you're up," she said. "Vi and Hannibal are back. We're meeting them at the diner in half an hour."

"Breakfast sounds great," he replied, stretching.

Her lips parted slightly, and he realized she was appreciating his muscular form.

He showboated just a little, stretching and flexing his muscles as she watched, looking hypnotized.

"I'll go tell Spenser," he said, getting up.

"Okay," she replied.

There was a moment of electric anticipation as he approached.

Fletcher restrained himself from acting, forcing her to make the first move, and only if she wanted to. Maybe last night he had merely been helping her soothe a need.

She moved toward him, went up on her toes, and kissed him gently but firmly on the mouth.

He pulled her close, kissing her patiently, thoroughly.

"Mm," he said, pulling back at last. "I'll see you in a few minutes."

She blinked at him and then smiled. "Yes, okay. Sure."

He headed down to his apartment with a spring in his step.

"We're going to the diner for breakfast with Vi and Hannibal in twenty-five minutes," he told Spenser, who was sitting at the table, scowling at another crossword puzzle.

"Really?" Spenser said. "That's all you want to tell me?"

Fletcher grinned.

"So, did she accept you, brother?" Spenser asked.

"No," Fletcher shook his head. "But I did not ask her to."

"So what were you doing all night?" Spenser asked.

"Bringing her pleasure," Fletcher said dreamily. "But mostly just holding her."

"Then she will accept you soon enough," Spenser said wisely. "But you have to ask her, or nothing will happen."

"Thank you, brother," Fletcher said politely. "You are

right, of course. I just want to give her space and time to be at peace with her decision. She had seemed so sure that she did not want the bond. I don't want to push her now that she seems to be considering it."

Spenser nodded and Fletcher dashed off to shower.

When he emerged a few minutes later, Spenser was already dressed and ready to go. They headed out of the apartment and met Jana in the hallway.

"Perfect timing," she said.

They all went downstairs together and out into the bright sunshine of the morning.

Stargazer was so cheerful at this time of day. Golden sunlight dappled the sidewalks through the changing leaves of the street trees.

A neighbor waved as she walked by with her dog. Shopkeepers tended to their storefronts, and kids with brightly colored backpacks waited for their bus at the corner. At one point, a group of older kids on skateboards nearly knocked them over, but they were all in good spirits, so no one seemed to mind.

When they arrived at the diner, Vi and Hannibal were already there and waved to them through the window.

"How did it go?" Jana asked Vi as they all sat down.

"It was a wild goose chase," Vi said, shaking her head.

"It was a *what*?" Spenser asked worriedly. He and his brothers had learned the hard way that the geese that visited the lake near the lab were not to be trifled with.

"That's an expression," Vi explained. "It means we didn't learn anything new. It was all for nothing."

"What are the chances of another antique purple Corvette Stingray popping up for sale at exactly the same time?" Jana wondered.

"Well, this wasn't exactly the same car," Vi said.

Jana looked at her quizzically.

"It was a toy," Hannibal explained.

"Yeah, he kept saying it was a miniature," Vi said. "Which is definitely a toy, not a real car. But it's why he posted about it in a way that made us think it was an actual car."

"He wanted to talk about his little cars a lot," Hannibal said.

"Yeah, we had to hear about them for hours," Vi said.

"We bought only one," Hannibal told them.

"You bought one?" Jana asked.

"Yes," Hannibal said, pulling something out of his coat pocket.

It was a very small and detailed purple car in a plastic display box.

"Amazing," Fletcher said, taking it and studying the little vehicle.

"Hang onto it for me?" Hannibal asked him.

"Sure," Fletcher said, tucking it away.

"Did you guys find anything?" Vi asked.

"The recon mission was a bust, too," Jana admitted.

"That's too bad," Vi said.

"You probably could have found the evidence you needed from a safe distance with a pair of binoculars," Jana said.

"Maybe not," Vi told her modestly.

"Anyway, Fletcher and I thought of another way to look for clues," Jana said. "And Spenser helped."

Spenser smiled and looked down at his hands.

Jana explained their plan to hide in the ice cream truck and get it towed to the shop while they were inside.

"A Trojan horse scheme," Vi said, nodding. "Nice. I don't think I've ever actually seen that done in real life."

Then Jana explained what happened next.

Fletcher noticed that she refrained from telling Vi about his special gift.

Though he would not have minded his brother's mate knowing his secret, he felt a warm gratitude that Jana was ready to protect it.

"Holy cow," Vi said when the story was finished. "Guys, what an amazing mission. Do you have the schedule with you?"

"I thought I'd better leave it home since it's important," Jana said. "We can look at it after breakfast - see if you can make anything of it. We certainly couldn't."

"Great job," Vi said, clapping her hands together delightedly.

"Well, we may be in even more hot water with Officer West than we were before," Jana said.

"Worth it," Vi declared.

Three waitresses appeared, carrying trays practically groaning with waffles, eggs, fruit, and toast.

"Thank you," Spenser said politely to each of them.

The table ate in friendly silence for a while.

Then Spenser looked up suddenly.

Fletcher followed his eyes.

At the register, Officer West waited for a table.

"Oh," Fletcher said.

"Holy crap," Jana said. "It's like we summoned her by talking about her."

Officer West looked over at just that moment. She almost did a double take.

"I guess we should go anyway," Vi said. "I'd like to get a look at that schedule."

"I'm just going to say hello to her," Spenser said, getting up from the table. "To be polite."

Vi and Jana exchanged a look.

Jana shrugged.

Fletcher laughed and Hannibal winked at him.

"No way," Jana whispered in awe.

"Wow," Vi said.

"Are you guys sure?" Jana asked.

"Well, no," Fletcher said. "But…"

They all looked at Spenser, who was leaning on the counter in a debonair manner, smiling at Officer West, who gazed up at him, looking both embarrassed and intrigued.

A waitress came and signaled for Officer West to follow.

As she walked away, Spenser got a sad look on his face.

"I guess we'd better put him out of his misery," Vi said drily. "Let's go."

12

JANA

Jana took a deep breath of the crisp fall air as they all stepped outside of the diner.

"Do you want to run a quick errand with me before we look at that ledger?" Vi asked.

"Sure," Jana said. "Where are we headed?"

"Town hall," Vi told her. "I have to submit my business name application for the next meeting."

"Great," Jana said.

"We're running an errand," Vi yelled back to the men. "We'll see you guys later."

They had all grouped around Spenser.

Hannibal gave them a little wave and Fletcher looked up at Jana as if he were a little disappointed to see her go. She gave him a little wave, and he grinned at her and waved back.

"Geez, get a room," Vi teased.

Jana laughed and wondered if Vi was going to ask her about Fletcher.

Vi was usually pretty businesslike. She was a great

friend, but she was always way more interested in asking Jana about her auditions than her dates.

"Have you heard from your agent yet?" Vi asked, as if she had heard Jana's thoughts.

"Not yet," Jana said.

"Is it driving you crazy?" Vi asked sympathetically.

"Not as much as I would have thought," Jana admitted.

"Well, you've got a fun distraction," Vi noted.

Jana glanced over at her.

"I mean our case, of course," Vi said.

"Your case," Jana corrected.

"You're the one who camped out in enemy territory trying to get evidence," Vi said. "It's not just my case."

"Do you have any guesses yet about who's behind it all?" Jana asked.

Vi shook her head. "This is a weird one. Hopefully, the ledger will give us some idea."

They reached Stargazer's town hall and Vi headed up the steps with Jana at her heels.

"How may I help you?" a receptionist asked them as they stepped inside.

Vi explained what she needed, and the woman pointed them down the hallway. They entered a small room with a counter and a few seats. The woman behind the counter smiled and asked them how she could help.

"I need to file my fictitious name petition," Vi said. "It's for my new business. I'm going to pay the ten dollars to expedite."

"I'm so sorry," the lady said. "But you should hold onto your ten dollars for a bit. The council isn't meeting this Tuesday."

"Why not?" Vi asked. "It's not a holiday."

"The Macro Foods people are here that day," the woman

explained. "Town council wants to accompany them on their site tour."

"That tracks," Vi said. "I guess I can wait an extra week."

Jana waited while Vi wrote a new check and turned in her form.

They were just walking out when a woman in a green suit saw them and smiled ear to ear.

"Oh my goodness, Violet Locke and Jana Watson," she exclaimed. "You found my little Fluffernutter. How can I ever repay you?"

Jana smiled back, realizing this must be one of the people whose dog they had found.

"It was nothing," Vi said modestly.

"It was *not* nothing," the woman said. "My nephew works for the newspaper, and he's writing a piece all about it. Can he call you for a quote?"

"Wow, sure," Vi said.

The lady took out her phone and Vi typed in her number.

"Thank you again," the woman said. "That whole experience was terrifying. I thought I'd never see Fluffernutter again. Though I must say," she looked around as if someone might be listening, then continued in a low voice, "he doesn't do his *you-know-what* in the *you-know-where* anymore, so that's one upside."

Vi nodded and they said their goodbyes.

"Where was her dog pooping?" Jana whispered to Vi as they headed outside, barely restraining a giggle at the thought.

"I have no idea," Vi said. "But he's not doing it anymore, so that's good."

"So weird," Jana said, shaking her head. "Who kidnaps someone else's dogs and then pays to train them?"

"It's quite a mystery," Vi agreed. "But not as interesting as the other mystery right under my nose."

"What's that?" Jana asked.

"Why were you and Fletcher looking so bright-eyed this morning?" Vi asked.

Jana laughed.

"What?" Vi asked.

"I was just thinking earlier that I love how you always ask about me first," Jana said, "rather than asking about guys."

"No offense to guys," Vi said drily. "But you're way more interesting."

"I wonder what Hannibal would say to that?" Jana teased.

"He doesn't count," Vi said with a slightly dreamy expression.

"Well, I like Fletcher," Jana said. "A lot. But I'm not rushing into anything. And he's being super cool about it."

"That's all I needed to know," Vi said.

And true to her word, she buttoned her lip and the two of them enjoyed a quiet walk home under the hazy fall sky.

13

JANA

Jana watched as Vi flipped through the pages of the towing company's schedule book.

"There's an appointment from the night the cars disappeared for B. Posey," Vi said. "Something about that name sounds familiar. But I don't know anyone named Posey in town."

"There was the Posey who married one of the original aliens," Jana suggested.

"I don't really see her being wrapped up in this," Vi said, shaking her head. "Besides, Posey is her first name."

"True," Jana said.

"What's the B for?" Vi wondered aloud. "Barbara, Bobby... Beauregard?"

"Beats me," Jana admitted.

"I just need to meditate for a little while," Vi said. "I'm going to play some DancyPants 3, and try to think."

Jana winced. Whenever Vi used the dancing video game of her own invention to concentrate, it was hard for anyone in earshot to concentrate on anything else.

"Don't worry," Vi said. "I have a mission for you and

Fletcher. Can you return a sound board to Bobby Meyer for me?"

"Isn't that one of the skateboard kids?" Jana asked suspiciously.

"Yeah, probably," Vi said. "He's got some garage band going, and he asked me to take a look at their soundboard. It just needed a little tuning up."

Vi pointed at a control panel-looking item in the corner of her room.

"Sure," Jana said. "Where does he live?"

"Over on the two hundred block of Elm," Vi said. "Green house, small front porch with a swing. By this time of day you'll be able to hear them practicing from the next street over. You won't be able to miss it."

"Okay," Jana said, grabbing the board. It was heavy but not awkward. "Good luck with the..."

But Vi was already wearing her headphones and attaching the sensors to her legs.

Jana shook her head and carried the sound board out of the room to find Fletcher.

Ten minutes later, they were driving down the two hundred block of Elm with the windows down.

It was a gorgeous day and just being close to Fletcher was intoxicating.

Jana tried not to overthink it, and just let herself enjoy the moment.

"There's a green house," Fletcher said.

There was no music, but Jana figured maybe the band wasn't practicing today after all. Vi didn't know *everything*.

They parked and knocked on the door.

A lady with a pretty purple head scarf answered. "Can I help you?" she asked.

"Hi there, Violet Locke sent us over with a sound board for Bobby," Jana said. "Does he live here?"

"Oh yes," the woman replied, eyeing Fletcher in that way that almost every woman did. Jana didn't blame her. "I'm his mom. I'm so sorry, dear, but he's not home right now."

"Vi thought he would be having practice now," Jana explained. "We can bring it in and set it up wherever he normally practices, if you want."

"Oh, hadn't you heard?" the lady asked. "The boys won that contest for the new practice space."

"They did?" Jana asked. That was an oddly specific contest.

"Oh yes," the lady replied. "The mayor came by with the keys and the prettiest little plaque. The boys were so excited."

"Where is the space?" Jana asked.

"Oh, it's about ten minutes out into farm country, but it's very nice," Mrs. Meyer said. "The boys are practicing there now."

"If you can share the address, we'll drop off the sound board," Jana offered.

"You don't need to do that," Mrs. Meyer said.

"It would be our pleasure," Jana told her.

She typed the address into her phone as Mrs. Meyer recited it, then they waved their goodbyes and were on their way.

The road out to the countryside was becoming very familiar, but it was fun to drive her own car after lumbering around in Vi's ice cream truck.

"Do you think Vi will find a clue in the schedule book?" Fletcher asked.

"One of the names sounded familiar to her," Jana said. "But she couldn't place it."

"I'm sure she'll figure it out," Fletcher said.

"Yeah, Vi is amazing," Jana agreed. "Best detective ever."

"I don't know," Fletcher said. "You were very daring last night."

She felt the blood rush to her cheeks, even though she knew he was talking about their adventure and not what he'd done to her in bed.

He touched her cheek very, very gently.

Suddenly, her chest was full of butterflies.

The driving directions on her phone dinged, and they parked in front of a small structure.

"I guess this is it," Jana said.

They got out of the car and unloaded the soundboard from the trunk.

Something didn't seem right. At first Jana couldn't figure it out, but after a moment, it seemed obvious.

"I don't hear anything," she said.

"Maybe they ended their practice early," Fletcher said.

Jana marched over to the door and knocked.

Nothing happened.

She pushed the button for the doorbell.

No sound issued.

"Oh well," she said.

As she turned to leave, the door opened and a wave of sound blasted out, loud enough to vibrate her teeth.

"Hey," the kid in the doorway said. "You brought our sound board."

She recognized him from around town, although she had never formally met him before.

The music stopped and the other kids piled into the doorway to grab the board from Fletcher.

"I'm Bobby," the first boy said.

"Vi says hi," Jana said. "And your new place is amazing. I couldn't hear a thing from outside."

"Yeah," Bobby replied. "It's totally soundproofed. That button you pushed isn't really a doorbell. It turns on a light to tell us someone is outside. It's because we make so much noise that we wouldn't hear the bell."

Well, he had a point.

"So you won this space in a contest?" Jana asked.

"Yeah, the contest Ricky entered us in," Bobby said.

"Not me, I think Pablo entered us," another kid, presumably Ricky, said.

"Nah, it wasn't me," a third boy said.

"Well, anyway, it's totally boss," Bobby said. "That's what they used to say back in your day, right?"

"Uh, sure," Jana said, trying to hide her smile. "You guys have a great practice, and congratulations."

They all waved and yelled, and Jana and Fletcher headed back to the car.

"Doesn't it seem weird that they won that building in a contest?" Jana asked.

"Maybe," Fletcher said.

But Jana knew it was probably outside of his limited sphere of knowledge.

"More importantly, why do none of them remember entering it?" Jana asked.

Fletcher just shook his head.

"Oh well," Jana said. "I guess I should just be happy for them. They seem like nice kids. When they're not zooming around town almost knocking people over with their skateboards."

14

FLETCHER

Fletcher watched the sunlight glitter in Jana's dark hair as they drove through the farmland, past the spread-out houses, and back into Stargazer village.

"Holy crap," Jana said suddenly, pulling the car into an empty spot a couple of blocks from home.

She leapt out of the car so swiftly he barely had time to follow.

He jogged after her and realized she was joining Vi, who stood with a gathering crowd of people who were all looking up at a giant mural on the brick wall of an apartment building.

"It's incredible," Vi said to Jana.

Fletcher looked up at the mural and almost did a double take.

He'd passed by the wall just yesterday, when the bricks had still featured the long-faded, peeling image of an astronaut floating in space. Local kids had added speech bubbles for the astronaut with spray paint over the years. Most of what the astronaut had to say was quite raucous. There were also what Jana called "tags" symbolizing various people or groups.

Now the surface was smooth and fresh as new silk, and the image was something wholly different. Something no one from earth should have been able to paint.

It was a view from his home world.

Aerie.

The bottom half of the wall was covered in ink-black crags and cliffs. The sky above was a familiar, electric-blue and dotted with a sea of stars.

In place of the astronaut was a man so physically perfect he could only be lab-grown. He was surrounded by a veil of mist, as if he were in the process of migrating into his new form.

The painting was so exquisite, so real, it almost seemed to Fletcher as if the stars were winking and the mist swirling around the masculine figure who so resembled his brothers.

Just trying to take it all in brought a tear to his eye.

"Who did this?" Vi was asking the other people thronged around the building.

But no one seemed to know.

In the lower left corner where a signature might have been, there was only a delicate white butterfly.

"I'll bet there's a Comic Con in Philly this weekend," Jana said knowingly.

"What?" Vi asked. "I mean, there is, but how did you know that?"

"Because I know who painted this," Jana replied with a smug smile.

Vi stared at her, clearly impressed.

"Wow," Jana said. "Is this what it feels like for you all the time, Vi?"

Vi laughed and rolled her eyes.

"You feel like taking a road trip into the city?" Jana asked Fletcher.

"Sure," he said.

"We'll go home and grab some snacks," Jana said. "Vi, there was something weird about Bobby's band rehearsal. It's probably nothing, but did you know they won some kind of contest and now they have a practice space out in the farmland?"

"Really?" Vi asked, stopping in her tracks.

"Yeah," Jana said. "Weird, right?"

"I'll look into it while you two head to Philly," Vi assured her.

Fletcher looked between the two women and felt glad his mate had such a good friend in her life.

He was beginning to understand that his close relationship with his brothers was something precious and unusual in this world of fiercely independent beings.

"Everything okay?" Jana asked, turning to him with a concerned expression on her lovely face.

"Everything is great," he told her.

And everything was.

15

JANA

Jana and Fletcher weaved through the big displays and colorful booths of the Philly Comic Con.

Jana wondered what this all must look like in Fletcher's eyes. There were hundreds of depictions of aliens here - from Dr. Who to little green men and everything in between. There were guys dressed up in muscle suits meant to look like the men from Aerie, and women in jumpers from every space show imaginable, not to mention the rest of the comic-book superheroes and villains, and the writers and artists who made it all up in the first place in the booths lining the aisles.

They were on their way to meet one of those artists, whose debut movie, based on her comic, was a critical and box office success.

At last, they rounded the corner past the Star Wars display and reached the center aisle.

Jana stopped in her tracks.

Yep, Beatrix was a success alright. The line to see her was literally out the door.

"So I used to know Bea," Jana told Fletcher. "And she's married to one of your brothers, Buck."

"He arrived before me on this planet," Fletcher said. "But perhaps he will recognize me anyway."

"Yeah, I'm sure you guys would know each other anywhere," Jana said. The men were so huge, and so attractive, it would be impossible for one of them not to recognize the other. But she guessed it might be a little more difficult when the last time you met, you were both made of gas and starlight.

"What do you mean you used to know Bea?" Fletcher asked.

"We went to the same summer arts camp one year," Jana said. "She was in graphic arts, and I was in theatre."

"Miss," a security guard said softly, "she'll see you now."

"Oh, we're at the back of the line," Jana said, wondering how Bea would have recognized her.

"She saw her brother-in-law was here, and wanted to say hello personally," the guard said. "You can go on ahead."

The women dressed like astronauts in line in front of them sighed, but the guard led them right up to the table.

"Hi," Bea said, extending her hand.

"Hey there, I'm Jana and this is Fletcher," Jana said, shaking Bea's hand.

"Jana Watson?" Bea asked.

"Yes, oh my gosh, you remember me?" Jana asked in wonder.

"*Own it, Jana,*" Bea cried. "And look at you - you're owning it!"

Jana beamed, suddenly forgetting why she was even there.

"So do you guys want to get together in a couple of days when the Con is over?" Bea asked. "Have a family dinner?"

"We would love that," Jana said.

"Here, write down your number," Bea said, handing her a Sharpie and a headshot. "I know, it's weird, but it's the only paper I have."

Jana laughed and wrote her number.

"There you go," she said. "There's something I really need to ask you, if you have one more minute?"

"Of course," Bea said.

"You did that gorgeous mural in Stargazer last night, didn't you?" Jana asked.

"That's an anonymous piece," Bea said with a wink. "But it sure looks like one of mine, doesn't it?"

"There's something strange going on in Stargazer," Jana said. "And I have a feeling the person who hired you may be able to help us understand what it is."

"Interesting," Bea said. "I wish I could help, but it was actually an anonymous request. The person gave a very generous donation to the foundation for art in schools that I volunteer with. I couldn't say no. I figured it was just someone wanting to make the town a prettier place."

"Wow," Jana said. "Did they tell you what they wanted it to be?"

"No," Bea said. "They said they wanted *a depiction for Stargazer's friends from far away - something to make them feel welcome and at home.* I knew they meant the men from Aerie, of course. I thought the cliffs would remind them of home, and of course the celebration of each brother migrating into human form, so they would know how lucky we feel to have them here with us, and how grateful we are that they let go of one way of life so that we could share another together."

Suddenly tears were prickling Jana's eyes, though she wasn't sure why.

Fletcher placed his hand on the small of her back and

she felt oddly comforted and somehow even more heartbroken all at once.

"Thank you, Bea," she said. "We'll go now, but call if you want to get together."

"Of course," Bea said. "See you guys."

Jana headed back into the crowd.

Fletcher grabbed her hand and held it tightly as they wove their way out of the pretend alien world and back to the very real one.

16

FLETCHER

Fletcher walked into his apartment to find his brothers had moved the coffee table to the side of the room.

The two of them were on their hands and knees on the living room rug, carefully putting posters into frames.

"Hello, brother," Hannibal said happily. "We liked the mural so much that we decided our apartment should have decorations as well."

Fletcher glanced at the posters. Each of them celebrated an eighties movie they had seen back on Aerie in preparation for migration into human forms.

These movies had been sent out far and wide as a welcome message from Earth. Humans had wanted contact with other beings.

But not Jana.

He sat on the sofa and put his head in his hands.

"What's wrong, brother?" Hannibal asked him, placing a hand on his shoulder.

"It's Jana," Fletcher said. "I think I messed things up."

"How?" Spenser asked.

"Things seemed like they were going well today," Fletcher explained. "I do not wish to ask her to give up her dreams. But today, it was like she thought she could have both."

Hannibal nodded. "We did some research, brother," he said. "Many actors have spouses. It is common that they marry and have families. Whatever it is that makes Jana think she cannot be an actor and have a family, it has nothing to do with requirements or propriety.

"Is that true, brother?" Fletcher asked.

"Very true," Spenser put in. "Search celebrity marriage on the internet and you will find numberless results. Some of them more heartwarming than others."

"She can have both a career and a relationship," Hannibal said.

"I would give her both, and happily," Fletcher said.

"She knows that," Spenser said suddenly. "I'm sure that she knows how much you care for her."

"I don't know," Fletcher sighed.

"What happened?" Hannibal asked.

"We went to a place called Comic Con," Fletcher explained. "It was most interesting, brothers, I wish that you had been there and that we could have spent a day exploring the humans' ideas of what it means to be alien."

"Yes, brother," Hannibal said. "One day we will go together."

"But then when we began talking with Beatrix, the artist who is married to our brother, Jana began to cry," Fletcher explained. "Well, she didn't cry, but as we walked away her eyes were full of tears. And she chose not to tell me why."

"Was this woman unkind?" Spenser demanded.

"Not at all," Fletcher said. "She was most welcoming. She asked if we would like to get together for a family dinner. It was clear how much she likes Jana. They knew each other in childhood."

"It sounds like a very enjoyable day," Hannibal said. "What do you think made Jana so sad?"

"I do not know," Fletcher admitted. "But I think that it was seeing another woman who was following her dreams," Fletcher said. "There was a very long line of very eager people there to see Beatrix. I'm afraid that Jana thinks if she accepts my bond her dreams will be lost to her."

"Spenser said something very wise just now," Hannibal said.

"I did?" Spenser asked, looking very surprised.

"Of course," Hannibal said. "You said that you were very sure Jana knew how Fletcher felt. But in my experience, humans are not as perceptive as our kind. It all comes of having a physical body. Bodies are very distracting. Sometimes you have to be very clear in your words to be fully understood."

Fletcher nodded, thinking.

"So he should tell Jana exactly how he feels about her, about her career, about everything?" Spenser asked.

"I would like to do that, but I wouldn't want to push her," Fletcher said.

"I am beginning to think that we worry too much about propriety," Hannibal said. "Your feelings for Jana are too important to be left unspoken."

"I should be her comforter in times of sadness," Fletcher realized out loud. "I should not have left her to run to Vi with her sorrows when I am here."

"Give her space to talk with her friend," Hannibal suggested. "You can help us hang up these posters while you think about what you want to say to her. When your idea comes to fullness, go to her."

"Thank you, brothers," Fletcher said. "I am glad we have each other."

"Yes, yes," Spenser said, sounding embarrassed. "Now help us decide which poster belongs over the fireplace. I believe it is the boy who is left alone in his house over the holidays. But Hannibal prefers the agency that defeats ghosts."

"They are the most fierce and ridiculous," Hannibal pointed out.

"Yes, but a holiday movie belongs over the hearth," Spenser declared.

Fletcher smiled as they continued their debate.

17

JANA

Jana paced outside of 221B, waiting for Vi to return.

All the events of the day were swirling in her head and she was too distracted to notice that the person walking up to her was not Vi.

She started forward and then realized it was one of the skateboard kids.

He was walking toward her slowly, without his board.

"Uh, hi," he said in a confused way, likely wondering why Jana had headed right for him.

She certainly didn't want to tell him she thought he was Vi.

"Where's your skateboard?" she asked instead.

"Someone took it," he muttered.

"Not cool," she said sympathetically.

He gave a sullen nod of acknowledgement and kept walking.

Vi appeared a moment later, carrying two greasy looking white bags and a cup holder with two paper cups, condensation running down their sides.

"Hey," Vi said breathlessly.

"What's all this?" Jana asked, her stomach practically growling in anticipation as the smell of deep-fried goodness hit her.

"Curly cheese fries and chocolate shakes," Vi said in a businesslike way.

"Wow," Jana said.

"You sounded stressed," Vi said.

"Touché."

They headed up to the apartment and Jana watched as Vi carefully set out the shakes and paper trays overflowing with fries.

"I talked to Bea," Jana said.

"Yeah?" Vi asked. "I was almost afraid you didn't get to her. She's really blown up since the movie came out."

"She's doing so well," Jana agreed fondly. "And the mural is definitely her work."

"Who hired her?" Vi asked.

"She doesn't know," Jana said. "Someone offered an anonymous donation to a foundation she volunteers for, so she agreed."

"Do you think we could convince the foundation to spill the beans?" Vi asked.

"Doubtful," Jana said. "If they start naming anonymous donors, they might not get the next donation."

Vi nodded in agreement as she shoved a cheese-covered curly fry in her mouth.

"So you did some digging about the contest for the studio space, right?" Jana asked, pulling her own curly fry slowly out of its pool of cheese, and letting it spring back into shape before taking a bite.

"Okay, here's the thing," Vi said. "I've dug everywhere I can think to dig. And I can't find one shred of evidence that there ever was a contest."

Jana took a sip of her heavenly milkshake.

The sweet chocolatey taste filled her senses and she had a moment of true contentment.

"Vi," she said dreamily. "Do you think maybe we're being silly?"

"What do you mean?"

"I mean even if it is all connected, someone trained the dogs, painted a pretty mural, gave some kids a studio space," Jana said. "It's weird but it's not exactly villainous."

"You forgot the stolen cars," Vi pointed out.

"True," Jana replied.

"And the skateboards," Vi added.

"What do you mean, the skateboards?" Jana asked.

"Oh, right, you weren't here," Vi said. "The community message board has been lighting up about skateboards going missing off of porches."

That lined up. She'd heard one of the kids complain about losing his right before Vi arrived with the food.

"What's happening in this town?" Jana asked.

"I have no idea," Vi replied. "And it's driving me crazy. I feel like it's right on the edge of my brain."

"Mm," Jana said, sipping her milkshake again.

"Oh wow, I'm sorry I keep forgetting to ask you," Vi said. "When do you find out about the play?"

Jana sighed.

"You know, I hadn't thought about it in like an hour."

Vi laughed.

"I know that seems silly," Jana admitted. "But it's all I've ever wanted, an opportunity like this."

"So you haven't heard?" Vi asked.

Jana shook her head.

"Is it weird that this thing with Fletcher has me wrapped up in knots?"

"Definitely not," Vi said. "But look at Hannibal and me. Did you really picture me settling down with a nice beau, like a week ago?"

"Definitely not," Jana laughed. "At least, not so quickly."

"In a weird way, that made it easier," Vi said thoughtfully. "Everything with him is so certain. It's all out in the open. I don't have to wonder where I stand."

That was a good point.

"How are you feeling about Fletcher?" Vi asked.

"I don't know," Jana admitted. "I like him a lot. But I made a promise to myself a long time ago that I would focus on my career until I got where I wanted to be."

"Does he know that?" Vi asked.

"Yes. No. Maybe?" Jana said.

"You can't toy with him, Jana," Vi said. "Not that I think that's what you're doing. But you have to be careful. They wear their hearts on their sleeve. Even if they look sooooo good without sleeves."

Vi smiled and popped another cheese fry.

Jana nodded and looked down at her hands, suddenly feeling horrible for letting anything happen with Fletcher. She hadn't meant to lead him on.

"When he says he would do anything for you, he means it," Vi said. "They don't just say *I would die for you*, like some of the guys we've known. Fletcher would launch himself in front of a moving bus in a heartbeat if he thought it would help you."

"I know," Jana said. "I know."

"Anyway, cheers," Vi said, lifting her shake. "To acting jobs and hot aliens."

"To friendship," Jana said instead.

"I'll drink to that," Vi said with a grin and then took a long sip of her shake.

18

JANA

Jana was just wrapping up a yoga session, inspired by her unhealthy lunch, when there was a tap at the door.

Vi had disappeared with Hannibal about an hour ago to check out the missing skateboard development, so there was no one else to answer the knock.

"Coming," Jana said, hopping up.

She opened the door to find Fletcher.

The afternoon light from the windows behind her made his eyes appear luminous. She wanted nothing more than to flow into his arms. But she remembered what Vi had said.

And she noticed the tension in his big body. He carried himself stiffly, as if he were nervous.

"Come in," she said, stepping backward to give him room.

She saw the flash of disappointment in his eyes, as if he had hoped she would embrace him instead of inviting him in like a hostess at a restaurant.

You're already hurting him, she scolded herself. *This is why you shouldn't have gotten involved in the first place.*

"Shall we sit?" she asked, feeling a stiff formality in her body as well, even though she'd spent most of the last hour stretching.

"Thank you," Fletcher answered.

He sat on the sofa and she perched on the chair opposite him.

For a moment, they observed each other, tension thick in the air.

She longed to break it with a giggle and then climb on his lap and cuddle into him, cheering them both up, before making slow, sweet love with him.

But that was the opposite of what she needed to do, the opposite of what a friend would do when they cared about the other person and didn't want to hurt them.

"Jana, I need to talk with you, seriously," Fletcher said. "Is that okay?"

Oh.

That sounded like a break-up.

Suddenly, stupidly, she wanted him more than ever.

She clenched her fists in her lap and nodded.

"Jana, I have loved every moment we've spent together," he told her, leaning forward, an earnest expression on his handsome face. "I feel lucky to know you and be part of your life."

"Me too," she said, knowing he expected her to say something.

"I want to allow you the time and space to decide what you want your life to hold," he told her. "But I also want you to know how I feel."

Her stomach twisted as she realized the conversation was going in the opposite of the direction she had thought.

"Jana, I love you," he said. "I want to be your mate. I

want to be your comfort in times of sadness, and your partner in joy. I want to protect and worship you."

She choked back a building sob.

"I want to be your husband, and the father to your children," he went on. "You are my whole world. And all I want is to make your world better."

"Fletcher, I can't," she whispered.

"Why not?" he asked. "Beyoncé has a husband."

"You know who Beyoncé is?" she asked.

"Of course," he told her. "Doesn't everyone?"

She shook her head and tried to clear her thoughts.

"Fletcher, I'm waiting to hear if I got a part that will send me to a tiny studio apartment in New York to rehearse," she said. "And if I don't get this part, I'll get the next one. Or I'll want to. At the end of the day I'm not ready to be a wife or a mother yet. I'm not ready to settle down in Stargazer and give you the mate bond you need."

His face fell.

"I am sorry—" he began.

"No, I'm sorry," she replied. "I'm sorry I can't be your mate. But I want to be a friend to you. And right now that means giving you some space so you can forget about me."

"I could never forget you, Jana," he said.

"And I will never forget you," she said, fighting tears. "But I hope that we can both move on."

She stood, hoping he would take the cue and do the same.

He did as she had hoped, and she walked him to the door.

"Jana, if you change your mind," he said.

"I won't," she assured him. It had to be a clean break. She couldn't keep him waiting in the wings. She respected and cared for him far too much for that.

He headed through the doorway, head hanging downward slightly. His whole physical demeanor seemed somehow smaller than before, as if the big man had shrunk while they spoke.

When he was gone from her sight, she closed the door again and leaned on it, wondering if the hollow feeling in her chest would ever go away.

19

FLETCHER

Fletcher walked out of Jana's apartment and down the stairs without thinking about where he was headed.

His feet automatically carried him past the second-floor landing and on down to the front door.

Outside, the air was clear and cold and the birds were singing with all their hearts. Scarlet leaves drifted down to join the golden ones that already lined the sidewalk. The rich scents of the dusky leaves and the aromas from the café across the street combined to create what Fletcher thought of as the essence of Stargazer.

But it all seemed empty.

He looked around. The world was still as lush and beautiful as before. It was Fletcher himself who felt bleak and barren.

He walked, not caring where he was going, passing the diner where he and Jana and their friends had enjoyed loud, delicious meals.

A few minutes later, he passed a bus stop and briefly

wondered if he should wait for a bus too, then board it and go wherever it took him.

But his feet kept going.

He saw a blur of other people out walking - mothers pushing strollers, groups of kids laughing and shoving each other, and a pair of men carrying basketballs and gym bags and talking animatedly.

He was surrounded by life, but Fletcher still felt alone.

At last, his feet stopped walking.

He looked up to find the mural of Aerie.

As the people on the sidewalk moved all around him, Fletcher stood perfectly still, a stone in a flowing river.

The mural looked so real. Stars seemed to twinkle and the mist around his transforming brother flowed like Fletcher remembered his own gaseous form used to flow.

He closed his eyes and pictured the peace of Aerie.

The silence there was absolute. And the contrast between the dark crags and the pure unfiltered starlight gave everything a depth that made this softly lit planet feel almost two-dimensional in comparison.

He remembered the weightlessness of his body, the way it had rippled and flowed in the winds of Aerie, the rich satisfaction of soaking in a bright ray of starlight, and the emptiness of an hour of darkness.

He had enjoyed a sort of wordless camaraderie with Spenser and Hannibal even then, before they had been chosen to migrate together into human form.

Fletcher had not been unhappy there. He had not known any other life and he had thrived in the vast quiet of his first world.

The alien in the mural seemed to glance up at him. For an instant, Fletcher was fixed in his terrible blue gaze.

That was when he recognized his brother.

This was not just any man from Aerie, it was Ash, who had such trouble migrating. In the end, he needed his bride to come to him in order to find the change. And when he finally did, the happiness they found among the stars knew no bounds.

He was an exception, but his story made Fletcher realize a staggering truth.

The mating bond wasn't about the place.

It wasn't about the distance or the geography. It wasn't even about bearing young.

It was about learning to be completely yourself by loving someone else with everything you had.

Even when it was hard.

Even when it hurt.

Fletcher had thought that the bond was about finding home, and it was.

But for Fletcher, home was where Jana was - no matter where that might be, and no matter if it was only ever the two of them.

"Things don't have to happen in a particular order," he murmured to himself. Things don't have to happen at all. I just have to love her. And I already know I can do that."

He headed dreamily back toward 221B, suddenly at peace with everything.

Jana was his mate. And when the time was right, it would be as clear to her as it was to him.

The sounds of other people's laughter and conversation warmed him now, making him feel a part of something instead of separate from it.

This was his world now too, because it was hers.

20

JANA

Jana tried to comfort herself by finishing her yoga routine, but somehow, she couldn't relax again.

All she could think about was the pain in Fletcher's eyes and the corresponding tearing she felt in her heart.

She had made the right decision. It wasn't acceptable to lead him on when she knew she would be unhappy in his world.

But it was impossible to imagine a lifetime without him. He had walked out the door only a few minutes ago, and it already felt interminable.

After twenty minutes of solid efforts to focus on yoga, she gave up.

Her mind was filled with thoughts of Fletcher - his gentle smile, the deep music of his laughter.

"What have I done?" she wondered aloud.

Her phone began to ring, as if in answer.

She slid it out of her pocket and picked up without even looking to see who it was.

"This is Jana," she said automatically.

"Hey, girl," a deep, friendly voice said. "It's Angie."

Jana's heart began to pound.

Angie was her agent.

"Hey, Angie," she said weakly. "How's it going?"

"I don't know," Angie teased. "How do you think it's going?"

"Good Lord, Angie, just tell me already," Jana exclaimed.

Angie laughed, wasting precious seconds.

"Okay, baby," Angie said, a smile in her voice. "You got the part."

The floor seemed to drop out from under Jana, and she practically fell onto the sofa.

"Really?" she asked.

"Really," Angie said. "They need you back in New York in a month to start rehearsals. Script is coming to you by courier in a day or two."

"Holy crap," Jana breathed.

"Holy crap is right," Angie agreed. "Congratulations. You worked hard for this, and you paid your dues for a lot of years."

"Thank you for everything you've done for me," Jana said, suddenly feeling weepy. "I know I wasn't the first person they thought of for this role. Thank you for believing in me and for kicking in the door to get me in front of them."

"That's why I get the big bucks," Angie laughed. "Go call the people you love. I'll email you the contract and we'll go over it when you're ready."

"Thank you," Jana said again, feeling totally shell-shocked.

Angie hung up and suddenly Jana was once more alone in the apartment with her thoughts.

She had done it.

She had worked hard to be the best she could be, and in spite of the odds stacked against her, she had found an agent who believed in her and ultimately landed a role that could change the trajectory of her career, of her whole life.

This was it - the amazing break she had prepared for since her teen years.

So why does it feel so empty?

She began to pace again, the room blurring around her as hot tears ran down her cheeks.

She didn't know if minutes passed or hours, but the door opened.

"Jana, what's wrong? What happened?" Vi demanded, dashing across the room to wrap her arms around her.

Jana let herself be embraced, feeling especially grateful since Vi was generally not a hugger.

"I-I... Angie called," Jana managed to say.

"Oh *no*," Vi said. "Well, fuck them. You're fantastic and it's their loss."

Jana smiled through her tears at her best friend's fierce loyalty.

"No," Jana said, letting go of Vi to swipe at her teary face. "No, I got it."

Vi pulled away, but kept hold of Jana's arms. "You got the part?"

Jana nodded.

"*Yes, you got it*," Vi cried, beaming. "So these are happy tears?"

"Yes and no," Jana said. "I just... I don't know. I don't feel like I thought I would feel."

"This is a huge, life-changing moment," Vi said, nodding. "It's natural to feel some trepidation."

Jana shook her head. "I have no fears about stepping up my career," she said. "I'm ready for that."

"So what's wrong?" Vi asked.

"I think... I think it's Fletcher," Jana said.

"Ah." Vi nodded, her expression showing she understood completely now.

"He came here after you left and I had thought about what you said earlier," Jana explained. "I do care about him and I don't want to hurt him. I told him we couldn't be together."

Vi nodded, wincing slightly.

"But now, I feel...broken inside," Jana said. "I've had bad break-ups before. This isn't like that."

Vi nodded.

"I'm beginning to think maybe he was right," Jana said. "Maybe we are already bonded. Maybe I can't leave him. Which means I have to call Angie back and turn down the part."

"Why?" Vi asked.

"Because I can't take him away from his brothers," Jana said. "He may look like a man, but he's like a baby in a lot of ways. He's new to this world and I can see how much he needs them."

"You've heard of this thing called a telephone, right?" Vi asked. "You just press the screen and there are all your friends and relations, talking to you like magic."

"He also wants to have children," Jana said.

"Well, so do you, one day," Vi pointed out.

"Sure, one day, but not now," Jana said.

"Did he say he wants them *now*?" Vi asked.

"I just thought, that was kind of their directive," Jana said weakly. "Aren't they supposed to come here and have families?"

"Think about how many of them there are now," Vi pointed out. "When there were only three here, it was important to prove they could connect with us, settle down with us. At this point I think you can buy yourselves some time."

"Maybe we could get a dog," Jana said thoughtfully. "They're like furry kids."

"*Holy shit*," Vi said, freezing.

"We don't have to get a dog," Jana offered. "Maybe just a bird or something to practice on?"

"No, it's not that," Vi said.

"What is it?"

"I know who's behind it?" Vi breathed.

"Behind what?"

"Behind *all* of it," Vi said.

"Who?" Jana demanded.

"No, no, come on, let's get the boys, we have to go, now," Vi said firmly, grabbing Jana's hand and heading for the door to the apartment.

21

FLETCHER

Fletcher ran to the door as someone on the other side pounded frantically.

"What took you so long?" Vi demanded, marching in with Jana in tow.

Jana gazed at him, her face tear-stained but exalted.

"Are you okay?" he whispered.

She nodded and gave him a tiny smile that sent shivers of joy through his blood.

"We're going to town hall," Vi announced. "Come on."

Spenser shrugged and followed her.

Hannibal jogged down the hallway from his room. "Vi?"

"Come on, brother," Fletcher said. "We are all going to town hall."

"Why?" Hannibal asked as they closed the door behind them.

"Don't bother asking," Jana said over her shoulder from the stairs below. "She won't tell us."

"You'll see soon enough," Vi said. "*Come on.*"

They must have made a funny picture marching down

the street in a group. People moved out of the way and a couple of tourists snapped photos.

Fletcher realized belatedly that this was exactly why Dr. Bhimani had asked them not to appear together in public. It was very clear that the people around knew they were from Aerie. The three of them together were just too big and too sexy by human standards.

But no one seemed unfriendly.

As a matter of fact, plenty of people smiled and shouted greetings. And a few began to follow them.

Ten minutes later, they strode up the marble steps of Stargazer's town hall, with a small crowd in tow.

"May I help you?" a receptionist asked.

"We're here to see the mayor," Vi said in a bright clear voice that rang against the marble floors.

"Do you have an appointment?" the receptionist asked in a nervous way.

"Oh, Blair, no one needs an appointment here," Mayor Harvey Smalls said as he strode out of his office with a big smile. But he did a double-take when he saw just how many people were waiting for him.

"Thank you so much, Mayor Smalls," Vi said. "But perhaps you'd like to talk with me privately?"

Fletcher looked around.

A few of the people in the crowd were holding up their phones to record the encounter.

"Uh, no," Mayor Smalls said. "This is fine. I've got nothing to hide."

"Is that so?" Vi asked. "Then why did you kidnap people's dogs to have them trained at your own expense?"

There was a collective gasp.

Fletcher and his brothers sometime struggled with proper expectations in human interactions, but even he knew that accusing the Mayor of a crime was the height of improper manners.

"I-I didn't do that," the mayor said.

Fletcher thought he looked very nervous, maybe too nervous to be telling the truth.

"What about the mural?" Vi asked. "Are you going to tell me you had nothing to do with that painting and the generous, anonymous donation that paid for it?"

The mayor shook his head, but his face was growing red.

"And what about the so-called contest for those kids with the loud garage band? Did you buy that space just for them?" Vi asked. "I'm guessing a search of the public record will give us that answer, even if you won't."

"I love this town," Mayor Smalls said quietly. "I only wanted to make it a better place."

"Then why didn't you make changes through the proper channels?" Vi asked. "You could have donated funds for the mural without being all sneaky about it."

"The process in this town is very difficult," the mayor said. "Things take so much time and so many committee members have their own priorities, it can be hard to get anything done. Remember how long it took to me get rid of those awful ice cream trucks? I worked for half a year to get that ordinance passed."

Yeah. Because only a monster doesn't like ice cream trucks.

"So you decided to skip the process, to go around the committees?" Vi asked.

"Everything I've done has been to help people and better this town," Mayor Smalls said, lifting his chin in defiance.

"What about the stolen cars?" Vi demanded. "What about the kids and their missing skateboards?"

There was a murmuring in the crowd.

"The cars are being restored at my expense," the mayor

said. "They will be returned. And the kids are getting their boards back on Wednesday, tuned up and better than new."

"Why Wednesday?" a woman in the crowd shouted. "My kid needs his exercise."

"Excellent question," Vi said. "Why Wednesday?"

"We know why," Jana broke in softly.

"We do?" Vi asked.

"On Tuesday, the Macro Foods exploratory committee is coming to Stargazer," Jana said loudly. "They're coming to look at our town and consider it for their new executive housing and campus. I looked it up online after the last time we were here."

"So on Wednesday, it doesn't matter if kids are skateboarding in the street again," Vi said, her eyes lighting up.

"Our town has a limited budget," the mayor said. "It's strained to the max now that we have so much tourism. The Macro Foods campus would be a boon for us. And the land they want is out in the farm country, so it won't congest the town streets."

The crowd began murmuring again.

Fletcher had to admit that it sounded like the mayor had a point. Though he had certainly gone about things in an odd manner.

"How did you figure it out?" the mayor asked Vi.

"Oh, a little clue you left for me," she said.

"What clue?" he asked.

"You made an appointment to have the cars towed," she said. "An appointment under an assumed name."

The mayor's face fell.

"Don't worry," Vi said kindly. "You're not the only person who's ever made a fool of themselves over a dog."

"B. Posey," Jana said.

"Exactly," Vi replied. "At first, I was searching for a person. Then it hit me. The mayor's dog. Barker Posey."

Fletcher blinked at Vi, amazed.

She really was a great detective.

"Okay, break it up, nothing to see here," a familiar woman's voice announced.

Fletcher turned to see Officer West striding through the crowd.

"Mayor Smalls, I'm afraid you need to come with me to answer a few questions, sir," she said to the mayor.

"Yes, Nat... Officer West, of course," he said meekly. "I'm so sorry, everyone. I really was just trying to help. I didn't mean to upset anyone."

She led him away as the crowd buzzed.

Fletcher watched as Jana turned, her eyes searching the faces in the crowd until she locked eyes with him.

A feeling of calm came over him as she walked over, a smile on her beautiful face. He couldn't' explain why, but he knew to his bones that things were going to turn out just fine.

22

FLETCHER

Fletcher walked beside Jana on their way home.

In front of them, Vi and Hannibal celebrated gleefully, with Spenser putting in a few words here and there.

Everyone was very proud of the work they had done. They had solved all the mysteries happening in Stargazer at once.

Best of all, the solution had been at least somewhat benevolent.

It was nice to know that the person behind the many strange happenings was acting out of altruism, not greed or malice.

For all that Fletcher had learned of the human race, it seemed that a certain degree of ruthless cruelty was always present among the people of Earth.

He was glad that no evidence of it had surfaced today.

"What an amazing day," Jana said, echoing Fletcher's thoughts.

"I've never seen Vi so happy," he agreed.

"This was a triumph for her," Jana agreed. "What an auspicious beginning for her new business."

"I don't think that's why she's happy," Fletcher said thoughtfully.

"Sure, I mean for her it's about solving the puzzle," Jana said. "It doesn't matter so much about the business."

"True," Fletcher agreed. "But that wasn't really what I meant either."

He watched Jana watching Vi, a more serious expression on her face.

"She's happy because of Hannibal," Jana said.

"And because of you, and because of all of us," Fletcher said. "It's good to have a family."

"Family," Jana said softly, as if she were testing out the word. "This isn't what most people think of when they think of family, but you're right."

"Jana, I made a mistake when I came to talk with you before," Fletcher said. "Would it be okay for me to say just one more thing to you about our bond?"

She turned to him, and he swore the expression on her face was relief. "Yes," she said simply.

He stopped walking and took her hands.

"When I came to you before, I talked about marriage and children," Fletcher said. "And those are things I would love for us to experience one day. But you should know that they are not necessary to me. Nothing is necessary to me, except being with you - in any way that makes you happy."

"Fletcher," she breathed.

"I traveled light years to be here," he went on. "A few hundred miles, or even a few thousand or a few million, could never matter to me. I would follow you to New York, or even back to Aerie and beyond, Jana Watson. I just want to be your family, to love you and have your back, for as long as you will have me."

She smiled up at him, tears streaming from her eyes.

"Jana," he groaned.

She went up on her toes and wrapped her arms around his neck, her soft, sweet body pressed to his, and kissed him like there was nothing else in her whole world.

When she pulled back, she was smiling again.

"Is that a yes?" he asked hopefully.

"It's a big yes," she whispered back. "I wanted to talk to you too, but I wasn't sure how."

"Come on lovebirds," Vi yelled back to them happily. "We're going to get some diner food."

"I think we're going to go home and talk for a while," Jana called back to her.

"I'll bet you are," Vi said, winking at her.

Jana looked embarrassed but she was still smiling. "See you guys later."

"We'll bring you back something," Spenser promised.

Hannibal gave Fletcher a friendly smile that told him he knew what was happening.

Fletcher grinned back, feeling like the luckiest being to have walked the surface of this strange and wonderful planet.

"Come on," Jana said, taking his hand and dragging him toward the door.

As soon as they were inside, she dashed up the stairs.

He chased her, laughing, and they exploded into her living room.

Jana stood in the center of the room, panting slightly.

"Now what?" he asked her.

But he knew what came next.

She approached him slowly, held out her arms.

Instead of embracing her he swept her up and carried her through the dining room and kitchen and into her bedroom.

He placed her gently on the floor and tilted up her chin.

"Are you ready to accept me as your mate?" he asked.

"Very ready," she replied, tugging at the waistband of his jeans.

He laughed and grabbed her wrists. "You first," he growled.

She helped him tear off her clothes, and watched in obvious anticipation as he peeled his shirt over his head.

"You're so beautiful," she murmured, running her palms down the planes of his chest, sending him nearly over the edge with her gentle touch.

"I am glad my form pleases you," he told her earnestly. "Yours pleases me very much."

He stopped undressing to kiss her again, slowly and thoroughly.

"Get in bed," he groaned, pulling back at last.

She crawled into bed as he kicked off the last of his clothes.

He paused for just a moment, gazing down at her.

Jana was so beautiful, with her lush body spread out on the bed before him like a feast. Her eyes hazy with need for him.

He hoped desperately that he could please her properly before taking her. His own need coiled in him, barely restrained.

"Fletcher," she murmured, arms out.

He climbed into bed and cupped her cheek in his hand, dipping his head down to kiss her lips lightly, a teasing brush.

Jana moaned and captured his lower lip in her teeth, nipping him gently.

The pleasure mixed with the tiny touch of pain, and he closed his eyes against an onslaught of desire.

When he opened them again Jana kissed him gently but passionately.

He could feel her trembling with need beneath him.

When they broke to take a breath, he rained kissed down on her eyelids, her cheeks, and then nuzzled her neck.

She arched her back as if craving closer contact.

He nibbled the tender flesh, wondering if she liked it as much as he did.

She rewarded him with a whimpering moan that sent shockwaves of need through him.

He kissed his way down to her breast, licking and suckling her sweet nipples until she sank her nails into his biceps.

He smiled and licked a trail down her belly. He could feel her relaxing her thighs open for him.

The first taste of her set his senses alight.

She moaned and gripped the sheets as he teased her tender sex.

With every caress of his tongue, he was torturing himself as much as her, as his own body raged to claim her.

23

JANA

Jana lay back, hands twisted in the sheets, losing track of her own sounds as Fletcher drove her closer and closer to the edge without letting her succumb to the pleasure.

"Please," she moaned at last.

Instantly the warmth of his mouth was gone.

She nearly screamed in frustration, but he was crawling up to her, caging her head in his arms, kissing her with his glistening mouth so that she tasted her own excitement on his lips.

"Please," she whispered.

"I love you, Jana," he told her, his voice raw with need.

When he entered her, there was a tiny pinch of stretching pain and then a wave of pleasure so intense that she clung to him, afraid she would be swept away by it.

Fletcher groaned and fed on her mouth again.

She wiggled beneath him and he pulled back and thrust into her again, moaning out his pleasure against her lips.

He moved slowly, deliberately, shaking as if with great effort to restrain his climax.

Jana jogged her hips up, urging him on.

He let go of his restraint and thrust furiously, again and again.

The pleasure lifted her higher and higher, like a helium balloon, a rocket ship, a planet, an exploding star.

She felt the moment when their bond was truly sealed and Fletcher clicked in to his human form for good. At that instant, she knew in her heart they would be together forever.

Then it all crashed down on her and she screamed out her ecstasy just as she felt him swell and jet inside her.

For a long time, the waves of pleasure settled over them, rocking them, and then the room seemed to fade back into focus.

The air was cool on her skin and she could hear the birds outside, chirping as they made a nest in the rain gutter.

"Jana," he murmured, rolling back and pulling her onto his chest.

"That was incredible," she whispered, shivering in his muscular arms.

"Let's never do anything else ever again," he suggested.

"The thing is though, Vi and Hannibal and Spenser are coming back here soon," she pointed out.

"Let them stay downstairs," he suggested carelessly.

"But they're bringing food," she said.

"Jana Watson, are you hungry at a time like this?" he asked.

"Yes," she admitted, her eyes twinkling.

"Well, me too, actually," he admitted with a grin. "Let's get ready to go see our friends. I think they'll be happy for us."

But instead of getting up, she pressed her lips to his, and felt the waves of need surging through her all over again.

24

JANA

Jana sat at the picnic table with her friends a few days later, watching the sun go down over the little trees that lined the walled garden.

In the yard, Maybelle scampered around with Tony, who was alternately throwing a ball for her and chasing her when she refused to bring it back.

Micah sat on his favorite lounge chair. His silk-kimono draped lap was uncharacteristically empty without Maybelle there to warm it, but he sipped a glass of lemonade and watched Tony play with her with a satisfied half-smile.

Hannibal had his arm slung loosely around Vi. They were bent over her tablet, trying to choose another case.

After the outing of the mayor's nefarious good deeds, Vi's services had been in great demand.

The local paper even did a small article about Locke's small hometown detective agency. Vi was quoted saying, *"I could never have done it without the help of my friends, especially Jana Watson."* Which made Jana feel a little weepy with joy.

"What about this one?" Hannibal asked. "*I believe my husband has been unfaithful.*"

"Let me see that," Vi said. "Oh yes, he's definitely been unfaithful, but we're not taking it."

"Why not?" Hannibal asked. "You already solved it."

"Exactly," Vi said. "It's boring. Besides, I don't like making people unhappy."

Hannibal laughed and kissed the top of her head as Vi bent over the tablet again, sliding her finger down the screen.

"Aren't extramarital affairs bread and butter for most PIs?" Micah asked.

"Maybe," Vi said. "But not me. I want something interesting."

"Don't we all, honey," Micah agreed.

"Really, I don't need to bring in enough to drape Hannibal in diamonds," Vi said. "We just need a case here and there to stay afloat."

"He might look nice in diamonds," Jana suggested teasingly.

"Hey, you've got your own guy," Vi teased back. "Don't think about draping mine in diamonds."

"True," Jana said. "But he's more of an emerald guy."

"Who's more of an emerald guy?" Fletcher asked, emerging from the back door with a plate of homemade hamburgers to put on the grill.

"You are," Jana said. "I assume."

"I prefer salt crystals," Fletcher said, laying out burgers on the grill. "They are attractive *and* delicious."

"You're a cheap date," Jana laughed.

"Not at the diner," he replied sadly.

"You can have all the pancakes you want," Jana said. "I'm a big star of the stage now."

"We're going to eat so much pizza in New York," he said dreamily.

"And so much Indian food and Thai food, and Ethiopian," Jana said, feeling a little dreamy herself. "It's like the whole culinary world, right at our doorstep."

"Will you tell us all about it, brother?" Spenser asked.

"You can come visit us," Fletcher said. "All of you can."

"Our apartment might be a little small for all that," Jana warned them.

"A little *cozy*," Fletcher corrected her.

"Did anyone ever tell you that you have the makings of an excellent Manhattan real estate agent?" Jana teased.

"That would be something constructive for me to do while you're in rehearsals," he mused.

"What about this one?" Hannibal said suddenly, pointing at Vi's tablet. "Macro Foods global conspiracy."

"Interesting," Vi said, frowning. "But most likely just another local nut job."

"Can someone grab the rolls for me?" Fletcher asked, flipping the first set of burgers.

Spenser hopped up and grabbed them from the picnic table. But instead of bringing them over to Fletcher, he stood in place as if he were frozen.

Jana followed his line of sight to find Officer West standing just inside the back door, wearing jeans and a faded tee shirt. It was odd to see her out of uniform.

"I... knocked, out front, but no one came," she said. "And the door was unlocked."

"What do you want?" Vi asked without getting up.

Officer West winced and Jana's heart went out to her. She moved to greet the woman, noticing the grateful look Spenser shot at her.

"Officer West, what can we do for you?" Jana asked.

"It's Natalie," she replied. "And... I can't believe I'm saying this, but I think I need your help."

"Why would a professional from the illustrious Stargazer police force need our help?" Vi asked scornfully. "I thought you guys wanted us out of the way."

"I'm not a part of the force," Natalie said softly. "At least not right now."

Everyone went silent for a moment.

"Okay, sweetheart," Micah said, rising slowly from his lounge chair like a sunrise. "This sounds like it's going to be a doozy of a story. Let's get some wine in you and hear it."

Natalie smiled at him. It was a lovely smile, and made Jana realize the other woman was younger than she had first thought.

"That sounds amazing," Natalie said.

Micah poured out wine and Tony and Maybelle joined everyone on the patio.

"Thank you," Natalie said, taking the mason jar of white wine and sipping.

Spenser sat beside her.

Jana noticed that for once he didn't look stiff or awkward. The gigantic alien looked like he was right at home.

"You're all very lucky to have each other," Natalie said, looking around at the people gathered.

Jana felt Fletcher's arm go around her shoulder.

She turned to him and the rest of the world began to fade away. Suddenly she didn't care about the burgers burning on the grill, or the former police woman who was suddenly looking to them for help.

The only thing in the universe that mattered was Fletcher and the way his eyes crinkled at the edges when he smiled at her.

"We'll be right back," Fletcher said. "I just have to ask Jana something really quickly."

"Seriously?" Vi asked.

"We'll ply our new friend with burgers and wine," Tony said quickly. "Give her a little time to get to know us before she spills her secrets. Go ask Jana whatever you need to ask."

He winked at Fletcher, and Jana swore he did it so she would see it.

So she would have a way out if she wanted one.

She didn't. But she would be eternally grateful to Tony for caring enough to give her one.

Natalie West was right. They were all lucky to have each other.

Fletcher led her out into the yard, to the back wall of the garden.

She could still see and hear their friends, who were deliberately puttering around on the patio, not looking at them.

"Jana," Fletcher said. "I am not asking you for babies or even for a pet."

"You don't want a pet?" she asked.

"I would love a pet," he admitted. "Maybe one of those really big cats with the feathery ears?"

"A Maine Coon cat?" she suggested.

"Yes," he said. "Do you like them?"

"Sure," she replied.

"Well I'm not asking for one," he told her firmly. "I'm asking for something else, something that's just about the two of us."

She nodded, knowing what was coming, but still feeling like she was on the edge of a precipice.

"Jana, before I knew you, I was lost," he said. "I no longer belonged to Aerie, but I was not of this Earth either. Now I belong. I belong wherever you are. You are my home."

He went down on one knee and held out a slender golden ring with a tiny shimmering stone.

"Jana, will you marry me?" he asked.

For one golden instant she saw her life with Fletcher spread out before her, and it was glorious.

She smiled and offered him her hand.

"Yes," she said. "Yes, I will."

He slid the ring onto her finger and then he was standing, wrapping his warm arms around her, lifting her up and twirling her around as their friends cheered.

There might be a lot of mysteries to solve in their future, and more than a little bit of commuting.

Life was full of uncertainties. But Jana knew she would never have to wonder about Fletcher.

His love was here to stay.

***

Thanks for reading **Fletcher**!

Want to see what happens when Fletcher's brother, Spenser, suddenly finds himself a LOT closer to Officer Natalie West?
Do you need to know if they will be able to keep their feelings for each other in check long enough to solve the murder that's rocked their small town to its core?
Just keep reading to get a sample of Natalie and Spenser's story...

Or grab your copy now!

Spenser: Stargazer Alien Mystery Brides #3

https://www.tashablack.com/samysterybrides.html

SPENSER - SAMPLE

1

NATALIE

In her dream, Natalie was stretched out on a fluffy towel. The warmth of the sun kissed her cheeks as the sounds and scents of gently crashing waves permeated her senses.

A gentle breeze skittered pleasantly across her skin.

She didn't remember booking a trip to the beach, which was her first clue that she was dreaming, but now that she was there, it seemed like a great idea.

Suddenly, she was aware of a presence.

She looked up and saw a shadow spill across her body - a man's shadow, all wide shoulders and narrow hips.

She shaded her eyes with her hand and turned to look up at the person who was interrupting her relaxation.

Her breath caught in her throat.

It was him.

Spenser.

The hunky alien was bare-chested, his muscular form glistening in the sun.

"Natalie," he said, his deep voice playing on her senses.

She opened her mouth but couldn't speak.

Spenser lowered his big body to hers, caging her in those huge arms. He gazed into her eyes as her body burned for him.

She swore she could see universes colliding behind those dark eyes.

When he closed them, she closed hers too, every nerve ending in her body focused on her lips, awaiting his kiss.

He pressed his mouth to hers and she felt it to her toes, the need pouring off him hotter than the overhead sun, stoking her own desperate desire.

A seagull cried somewhere nearby, and then another.

She tried to focus on Spenser's mouth, and ignore the rhythmic calls.

But they only grew louder as the pressure of his body on hers began to fade away.

She tried to pull him closer, but he melted under her touch.

Natalie woke up at last, squinting into the early morning light with a handful of sheets, her alarm clock blaring beside her.

"Damn, Nat," she muttered to herself, reaching over to slap the alarm clock off. "You seriously need to get out more."

She staggered to the bathroom, suspecting that a hot shower, followed by a cup of coffee and some breakfast would do a lot to ease her morning funk.

Filling her belly would be easy. Filling the emptiness left behind by her dream of romance might prove to be a little more difficult.

Natalie hadn't exactly been active on the dating scene lately. She had spent so much time focused on her career, that she wasn't sure she even remembered how to date.

"Who cares?" she muttered to herself. "Men are trouble anyway. You don't need one."

Which was true. She didn't need one.

But she kind of wanted one.

Maybe she should get a dog instead. She'd been thinking about it. They were big and slobbery, just like men. She wasn't sure how her landlord would feel about it, and paying a dog walker for when she was at work wasn't cheap. But maybe it was worth it if a little companionship from a loyal pet would keep her out of trouble.

Or maybe she didn't need *that* much help keeping her mind off men. After all, the man she was dreaming about wasn't even technically a man at all.

He was an alien. Which had its own baggage. But the real issue was that he was the brother of the alien mated to that dreadful Violet Locke, who was always interfering in police business and generally making a nuisance of herself. That whole group over on Crescent Street was trouble, and the last thing she needed was to be head over heels in helpless lust with one of them.

"Nope, nope, nope," she said to herself as she slipped under the steaming water.

But she suspected it might be too late for her.

She had talked with Spenser twice. Each time the air between them seemed to shimmer with the magnitude of their mutual lust.

She had walked away shaken both times, and hadn't been able to think of much else for a long time afterwards.

"Focus," she told herself. "Could be a big day today."

The chief would be announcing the new Community First task force today.

Natalie loved the work she did with the kids in the community, both on duty and off. She knew she was young to head up a task force, but it felt like a great fit. And even if she didn't get chosen to lead, the mere existence of the task force in the first place would be the culmination of a lot of lobbying on her part.

"A big day, no matter what," she congratulated herself as she finished up her shower and headed back to her room to get dressed.

A few hours later, she was ensconced at her desk, a cup of coffee in one hand, and a phone in the other.

"What kind of cat is it?" she asked.

"I don't know, just... a black one," the lady on the other end said anxiously.

"A kitten? An older cat?" Natalie asked, jotting down notes.

"I guess kind of like a teenager," the woman replied, sniffing. "I just got him at the shelter last week."

"Like a young cat?" Natalie asked.

"Yes," the woman said.

"Is he wearing a collar?" Natalie asked.

"No, I want him to be able to chase mice," the woman said. "So I didn't put anything noisy on him."

Natalie managed to stifle her desire to give a lecture on why pets needed collars. The lady was clearly seeing the error of her ways.

"Is he micro-chipped?" she asked instead.

"Yes, he has a chip," the lady replied.

"That's great," Natalie praised her. "It was really smart for you to do that. And I'll bet when we find him we can find a lightweight collar that won't slow him down when he's chasing mice, right?"

"Yes, officer, absolutely," the woman promised.

"Don't worry, we're going to do all we can to track him

down," Natalie told her. "And I will reconnect with you by the end of the day one way or the other."

"Th-thank you," the woman sniffed.

"That's my job," Natalie told her.

They hung up, and Natalie headed to the break room to refill her coffee. It was going to take time to call all the local shelters. If that didn't work out, she'd head over to Arbor Avenue and search on foot.

She thought bitterly about the time she'd wasted trying to find the last crop of lost pets, when it turned out her own mentor had rounded them up and taken them for training without telling anyone.

Harvey Smalls was a good mayor, whose heart was absolutely in the right place. And he was usually a great mentor, especially since Natalie didn't have much support from her family. She had no siblings, and she wasn't close with her parents, so she appreciated the guidance she got from Harvey all the more. And he was usually right on the money with his advice, both career and personal.

But she had to admit that his recent efforts to single-handedly make Stargazer into some kind of model town had been a bit misguided, at best.

And Natalie wondered if fewer skateboarders and barking dogs would really make any impression at all on the big corporation that was coming to Stargazer to look at opening an executive campus in town.

She shook her head as she poured out another cup of joe.

"Busy morning?" Lance, one of the other officers asked.

She wasn't really what you would call close with any of her coworkers, but Lance was probably the one she would be most likely to call a friend. He was kind, and seemed to like the job almost as much as she did.

"Lost cat at 108 Arbor Avenue," she told him.

"What color?" he asked.

"Black," she replied. "Young cat, male."

"Hey," Lance said. "Do you think that could have anything to do with the black cat those people found at 110 Arbor Avenue?"

"Do I think the lost cat at 108 has anything to do with a found cat at 110?" Natalie asked, laughing. "Yeah, I'm pretty sure it does. What's the name of the homeowner at 110 again?"

"Lemme check," Lance said.

She followed him to his desk.

"It's Nuñez," he told her, reading his notes. "I'll call them."

"Nah, it's my lunch break anyway," Natalie said. "I'll stop by on my way to Burger Planet."

"Suit yourself," Lance said.

A few minutes later, she drove down Arbor Avenue and pulled over in the shade of a scarlet leafed street tree.

When she stepped up onto the porch of 110, she could hear the happy sounds of children squealing over something, presumably the neighbor's cat.

She rang the bell.

A man opened the door, he was carrying a half of a peanut butter sandwich. A small toddler in a rainbow dress clung to his leg and looked up at Natalie with wide eyes.

In the background someone was chanting, "*Cat! Cat! Cat!*"

"Are you here about the cat?" the father asked hopefully.

"I'm here about the cat," she confirmed.

"Thank God," he said.

The chanting child appeared with the other half of the

peanut butter sandwich. She looked nearly identical to her sister. This poor guy had more than he could handle.

A small cat trailed in the child's wake, appearing to be more interested in the sandwich in her hand than in the girl.

"Who does it belong to?" he asked.

"Would you believe me if I told you it lives next door?" she asked.

He threw his head back and laughed.

"She just got it last week," Natalie said, smiling. "Do you want me to bring it over?"

"No, no, the girls and I will bring the cat back to its owner, right girls?" he asked hopefully.

The girls took the news with good cheer, but in fairness, they probably didn't know what he was talking about.

Natalie headed back out to her car and watched as the dad carried the cat over to the house next door, toddlers in tow, and presented the missing feline to its very grateful owner.

He waved to Natalie on his way back home with the kids.

"Thank you so much, Officer West," the cat's owner called to her tearfully.

"My pleasure," Natalie called to them. "You all have a great day."

Moments like these were the best part of the job. Unlike some of her colleagues, Natalie hadn't gotten into this line of work for over-the-top excitement of any kind. She loved her town and wanted to help.

She hopped back in the car and had almost made it to Burger Planet when her radio crackled to life.

"Hey Merle," she said.

"They need you over at the mayor's house," Merle said

in a worried voice, abandoning any attempt at police jargon and just sounding like a person in distress.

"What's up?" Natalie asked.

"Just get there as soon as you can," Merle said, clicking off.

2

NATALIE

Natalie stood in the mayor's study, a pleasant, shadowy room where she had spent countless quiet hours talking with her mentor about her dreams for the community.

Today, the brocade drapes had been thrown open to let in muted sunlight from the shaded patio on the other side of french doors.

It would have been pretty, except that the prone, lifeless body of Harvey Smalls lay on the floor behind his desk.

Natalie wrapped her arms around her shoulders and willed herself to breathe.

"This looks open and shut to me," Chief Roberts said. "He had a known allergy. There's an open container of food on the desk. Looks like he just didn't have his epipen handy."

"He always had it handy," Natalie said automatically.

"Well, maybe not handy enough," the chief replied.

"Check the top desk drawer," Natalie said, turning to look out the french doors and into the mayor's idyllic backyard to try and center herself.

She could hear someone rummaging around in the desk behind her.

"Nothing in here, Chief," Lance said.

"That can't be right," Natalie said. "He always kept one near him, always. He was incredibly careful about his allergy."

She stepped over and looked in the drawer herself.

Lance was right. There were sticky notes, pens and pencils, and a few papers. But there was no epipen.

She sighed.

In the next room, she could hear a low, animal whine.

"Barker Posey," she said, remembering the mayor's beloved dog.

"We put her in her crate," Lance said. "She was kind of freaking out."

Of course she was. The poor thing was probably confused and terrified. Natalie was feeling a bit of both herself.

"I'll take her home with me," Natalie said. "Is that okay, Chief?"

"Sure," the chief replied. "It's that or the shelter. He doesn't have any family nearby that I know of."

"Look, I'm going to deal with the dog for now," Natalie said. "But please, promise me we'll keep this case open. Harvey would never have eaten a bite of something without checking for nuts. And he definitely wouldn't have been without an epipen. And the food right on the table, that feels too convenient to me. There's something fishy about all of this."

"Natalie," the chief said. "Walk with me."

She allowed him to take her arm and walk her down the hall to where the mayor's dog shivered in her crate.

The enormous Saint Bernard looked almost small with

fear. She gazed up at Natalie, her dark eyes filled with sadness.

I hear you, girl.

"Listen, I know how much the mayor meant to you," the chief said kindly. "No one would blame you for having big feelings on this. But it's clearly a terrible, tragic accident."

"But Chief—" Natalie began.

"I'm going to have to ask you to let this go," the chief said. "We're not going to investigate this as a force, and I'm asking you not to investigate it on your own. You're not thinking clearly right now, but I know you care about this community. You wouldn't want to upset everyone over something that's clearly not a murder."

When he used the word *murder* it gave her a moment of pause. She had been thinking there was a little more to it. But would someone really *murder* the mayor?

"To make it easier on you, I'm giving you a week off with pay," the chief went on. "Take some time and mourn. We'll be here when you get back."

"Thank you," she heard herself say. Her voice sounded far away.

"This force is a family," he said, thumping her once on the back. "Call if you need anything. And try to get some rest, and remember to eat. Margaret will stop by with a casserole."

Margaret was the chief's wife. She was famous for her numerous, inedible casseroles. And for her warm hugs.

"Thank you," Natalie said again, grabbing Barker Posey's leash. "I'll just get her out of here."

Thanks for reading the sample of **Spenser!**

Want to see what happens when Natalie turns to Spenser and his friends for help with the case? Want to know if they can restrain their growing desires long enough to get to the bottom of it before it's too late?

Then grab your copy NOW!

Spenser: Stargazer Alien Mystery Brides #3

https://www.tashablack.com/samysterybrides.html

TASHA BLACK STARTER LIBRARY

Packed with steamy shifters, mischievous magic, billionaire superheroes, and plenty of HEAT, the Tasha Black Starter Library is the perfect way to dive into Tasha's unique brand of Romance with Bite!
Get your FREE books now at tashablack.com!

ABOUT THE AUTHOR

Tasha Black lives in a big old Victorian in a tiny college town. She loves reading anything she can get her hands on, writing paranormal romance, and sipping pumpkin spice lattes.

Get all the latest info, and claim your FREE Tasha Black Starter Library at www.TashaBlack.com

Plus you'll get the chance for sneak peeks of upcoming titles and other cool stuff!

Keep in touch...
www.tashablack.com
authortashablack@gmail.com

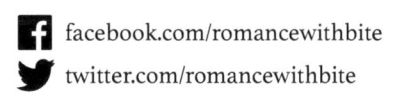

facebook.com/romancewithbite
twitter.com/romancewithbite